Janny,

SEAL LOVE'S
LEGACY

Silver SEALs Book 1

SHARON HAMILTON

Sharon Hamilton

SHARON HAMILTON'S BOOK LIST

SEAL BROTHERHOOD SERIES
Accidental SEAL (Book 1)
Fallen SEAL Legacy (Book 2)
SEAL Under Covers (Book 3)
SEAL The Deal (Book 4)
Cruisin' For A SEAL (Book 5)
SEAL My Destiny (Book 6)
SEAL Of My Heart (Book 7)
Fredo's Dream (Book 8)
SEAL My Love (Book 9)
SEAL Brotherhood Box Set 1 (Accidental SEAL & Prequel)
SEAL Brotherhood Box Set 2 (Fallen SEAL & Prequel)
Ultimate SEAL Collection Vol. 1 (Books 1-4 / 2 Prequels)
Ultimate SEAL Collection Vol. 2 (Books 5-7)

BAD BOYS OF SEAL TEAM 3 SERIES
SEAL's Promise (Book 1)
SEAL My Home (Book 2)
SEAL's Code (Book 3)
Big Bad Boys Bundle (Books 1-3 of Bad Boys)

BAND OF BACHELORS SERIES
Lucas (Book 1)
Alex (Book 2)
Jake (Book 3)
Jake 2 (Book 4)
Big Band of Bachelors Bundle

TRUE BLUE SEALS SERIES
True Navy Blue (prequel to Zak)
Zak (Includes novella above)

NASHVILLE SEAL SERIES
Nashville SEAL (Book 1)
Nashville SEAL: Jameson (Books 1 & 2 combined)

AUDIOBOOKS
Sharon Hamilton's books are available as audiobooks narrated by J.D. Hart.

ABOUT THE BOOK

A thrilling race against time haunted by loss and love from the past.

Former SEAL Commander Garrett Tierney must stop a crazed cult leader planning a Doomsday event, targeting the President's family. He leads a new DHS multi-agency task force, (Bone Frog Command), created to take on threats to the homeland.

The future of this task force is on his shoulders, as he dusts off the cobwebs of his retirement. Commander Tierney is tasked to work with a civilian—a young woman who is the daughter of his best friend, a fallen Teammate who died in his arms.

As their chemistry grows to explosive proportions so does the evil cult leader's devilish plans. Will Tierney have to sacrifice himself to save his new love and the honor and lives of the men and women on his new team?

AUTHOR'S NOTE

I always dedicate my SEAL Brotherhood books to the brave men and women who defend our shores and keep us safe. Without their sacrifice, and that of their families—because a warrior's fight always includes his or her family—I wouldn't have the freedom and opportunity to make a living writing these stories. They sometimes pay the ultimate price so we can debate, argue, go have coffee with friends, raise our children and see them have children of their own.

One of my favorite tributes to warriors resides on many memorials, including one I saw honoring the fallen of WWII on an island in the Pacific:

> "When you go home
> Tell them of us, and say
> For your tomorrow,
> We gave our today."

These are my stories created out of my own imagination. Anything that is inaccurately portrayed is either my mistake, or done intentionally to disguise something I might have overheard over a beer or in the corner of one of the hangouts along the Coronado Strand.

I support two main charities. Navy SEAL/UDT Museum operates in Ft. Pierce, Florida. Please learn about this wonderful museum, all run by active and former SEALs and their friends and families, and who rely on public support, not that of the U.S. Government. www.navysealmuseum.org

IF YOU GOT ANY CLOSER, YOU WOULD HAVE TO ENLIST

I also support Wounded Warriors, who tirelessly bring together the warrior as well as the family members who are just learning to deal with their soldier's condition and have nowhere to turn. It is a long path to becoming well, but I've seen first-hand what this organization does for its warriors and the families who love them. Please give what your heart tells you is right. If you cannot give, volunteer at one of the many service centers all over the United States. Get involved. Do something meaningful for someone who gave so much of themselves, to families who have paid the price for your freedom. You'll find a family there unlike any other on the planet. www.woundedwarriorproject.org

CHAPTER 1

GARRETT TIERNEY, U.S. Navy SEAL Commander (Ret.), was having a good day mucking out his chicken coops on an especially warm, autumn afternoon in Northern California. Even his eight-year-old rooster—the meanest animal he'd ever met—had left him alone. Maude, sold to him as a pullet with the two-dozen other Americanas for his new free-range egg venture, would normally be attempting to stab him in the calves after taking a flying leap several feet into the air. Garrett vowed one day he'd put a shovel to his neck. It wasn't his fault the bird was misnamed, but he figured Maude saw it otherwise.

He wore his knee-high muck boots just in case.

His handyman, Geronimo, hauled the manure-filled wheelbarrow to the acre vegetable patch Garrett lovingly tended. They were going to plant some new curly-leaf Kale and red cabbage starts in the mixture later, before sunset.

Tierney rested a bit on his shovel, feeling the strain in his lower back from an old injury occurring on one of those midnight HALO jumps in Afghanistan years ago. At forty-four and holding, his body was still as strong as some of the young froglets, or new Team Guys, he occasionally saw. Except for his back. But he could live with that. In fact, he was damn proud of it.

He surveyed his ten acres, all flat and useable, with the small winter creek going through the lower boundary that would fill up soon and need some repair work. It was a nice little slice of Heaven, tamed and carved out of the old apple orchard long since gone. He'd used some of the old wood to make rustic cabinets and countertops inside the bungalow he and some friends had built.

Geronimo returned with the red wheelbarrow.

Tierney always spoke English to the man. "I think maybe we got two more to go. Then I can start spreading shavings."

"Your garden looks good, Commander. You plant just in time. We got rain coming tomorrow," he said, pointing at the bright blue sky being invaded by large, grey puffy clouds.

"Perfect!"

He was spreading pine shavings and adjusting the chicken boxes inside the night coop when he heard the phone ring inside the house. No one ever called him on that line, except for telemarketers, so he let the answering machine pick up.

The hens began jockeying for position, scratching the floor and testing their butts in the new shavings. Maude chased several of them and scored with three, one right after the other. He laughed at the rooster, who stopped and angled his head, as if listening to him.

"You know what they say, Maude, a little more foreplay and less rape? It would make for a nicer hookup. You don't have to sweet talk them, but the jumping on their backs, biting their necks, and running their faces into the mud, that's not cool."

But what the hell do I know? He'd had his share of girlfriends, but nothing stuck.

Maude looked in the opposite direction and crowed, flapping his wings and getting as tall as his twenty inches could get him. If he behaved himself, he might die a natural death, as Tierney let most his senior hens do. He kept a side yard for the older girls where Maude couldn't get them.

Tierney enjoyed chatting about chicken sex with Maude, because it was a one-way conversation, which is what any conversation on sex should be, he thought.

He'd done it all in his twenty-five years in the Navy. Went in as a dumb kid right out of high school, made it through BUD/S, did five back-to-back tours on two Teams. When he almost got in trouble, he was recommended and went to OCS and still actively deployed. He'd never wanted to be anything but a Master Chief, but the Navy had other plans. Because of his extensive combat experience, Tierney was one of the most respected amongst his peers as he rose to the rank of Lieutenant Commander.

But now I'm still a dumb kid. An older dumb kid.

Geronimo had asked him recently why he never got married.

"You *do* know it isn't the man's choice, right? I never got married because no woman ever chose me."

They'd had a good laugh at that.

Life was pretty perfect. If it wasn't for his back. He bet he could still bark orders and make men pee themselves, run faster than the tadpoles, and qualify expert if he tried, though. The way Tierney figured, he'd seen enough of the world in his first twenty-five years of adulthood. Now it was time to quit running things and start just living with the rest of it.

Of course, there was always something to fix—some issue with the well, the septic system, fencing, or his solar panels. Something needed paint, something broken on one of his tractors or splitters or his beat-up farm truck, an issue with the plumbing, or a light that wouldn't work. That kept him pretty busy.

At night, he'd read or crash on his huge leather couch that fit him like a second skin, watching old war movies because it helped him sleep. He had his half-Doberman, half-Pit Bull rescue dog, Snooker, and a litter of cats in the barn he could never catch, who kept the mouse and rat population at bay.

He needed a woman like he needed a second dick. She'd just get in the way.

But on some of those cold, dark evenings, he missed the Brotherhood, if he was totally honest with himself. He could do without the bleeding and dying. But accomplishing the missions and saving some innocent lives, or one of his own guys? That shit was fun. Making it out alive just in time and blowing stuff up, he could do that until he was eighty, maybe longer. His sister had called him an old Boy Scout. Well, that's how a woman thought.

And that's why he was still single.

GARRET HAD JUST stepped out of the shower when he heard his phone ring. Wrapping himself in a bathsheet, he padded barefoot to the kitchen, checking the windows for any evidence of outside visitors. He thought Geronimo was long gone, but sometimes, his helper would work late sharpening the gardening tools in preparation for the next day's chores.

He waited, never answering without knowing who was on the other line first. Those who knew him understood this. Those who didn't, well, they shouldn't be calling his home phone.

"Come on, Tierney, you asshole. Pick up."

He recognized the voice immediately.

"Commander, what can I do you for?" Holding his breath, he knew it wasn't a social call. Former SEAL Commander Silas Branson was not one to chit-chat. And he knew the world had to be at an end before he ever would get a call from him.

"I'm with DHS now, and I got something you might be interested in."

Tierney didn't say a word, exhaling with control so Branson wouldn't detect he was working on his nerves. He inhaled again, holding his breath until dark circles started appearing in his eyes.

"Tierney? You there?"

"I'm all here, Commander. What I didn't leave over in the sandbox."

"You came out better than most."

"And that's a fact. Now what could possibly interest me more than getting drunk on a beautiful California sunset, working in my garden, gathering blue and green eggs, planting my three dozen veggies in the morning, and then maybe getting laid before sunset?"

"That's a tall order. But there was a time when your country came before all that."

He didn't know what to say, because anything that might pop out would be disrespectful of the good old

U.S. of A., to Commander Branson, or to himself. So, he waited. But it pissed him off no end. It was one of those wounds that woundn't heal, like he didn't deserve his time off after what he'd seen in the theater of war.

"I'll take that as a yes," Branson mumbled.

"Yes, what?"

"Yes, you're interested."

"And how the hell did you get that?"

"Because you would have hung up on me, that's how."

AFTER THE PHONE call, he shuffled back to the bathroom with the wet bath sheet still draped across his hips like he was some Roman Legionnaire at a bath in Carthage. He examined himself in the partially fogged mirror. He knew he looked old. His lines were the same, but deepened, especially the ones around his eyes and mouth. He had some grey hair making a showing at his temples some woman had recently said looked sexy. He didn't think so but was against altering the natural color of his hair.

If God made it, I'm gonna wear it.

His hands didn't shake anymore, like they did the last year he served on the Teams. He knew that was from getting more sleep than he'd ever gotten before in his life and from all the outdoor work he did. Building the house had been good for him. Tilling the soil had brought him back to life. Rescuing Snooker from the shelter was the cherry on top. He had his land, his dwelling, and, with Snooker, he had his family. He was taken care of and could just live this way until he was ready to check out.

He was *not* ready for another mission. He didn't have to prove to himself or anyone else he had what it took, that he could still outrun those little froglets and eat and drink them under the table.

So then why in God's green earth had he said yes?

THE TICKET HAD arrived online like Branson said it would. Two days later, he disembarked from the flight to D.C., meeting in a "need to know" location somewhere in the bowels of the city. Stepping out into the terminal, it smelled the same. The mix of races and body sweat overpowered him. The pace was faster than he was used to. Everyone was so busy, each with their own agendas. Some were harmless. Most of them in D.C. were dangerous, at least for those who had to go do the work the Head Sheds of government manufactured.

Commander Branson was a cool dude with warm brown eyes. He was disarming the way those eyes could look so sad. He'd lost his son not more than three years back. Garrett knew what it was like to lose family. But losing a child might be something a man couldn't ever get over. Every time he looked at Branson, he saw the pain the man tried so hard to cover up.

But what really stood out was that Branson had bulked up. At 6'3", he'd always been one of the big guys, but now he looked like a fuckin' transformer. His small waist and broad shoulders were tight, without an ounce of extra fat anywhere. Cut and lean, Garrett guessed the man still weighed 220.

He leaned against a shiny black Ford F-150 Raptor, and the Military Model to boot. No mistaking the fact that Silas wasn't into hauling soil or chicken feed or pulling a trailer or tiller out in a field somewhere.

"Son of a bitch, Commander, you haven't aged a year since we last saw each other. You on steroids?"

"Nah, don't touch those things. Besides, you were drunk, Tierney, and you had that little muffin top on your arm, the one with the—" He demonstrated the size of the bridesmaid's upper torso.

"Shut up." Garrett never was apologetic he loved girls with curves, the more the better, as long as they could be athletic in bed. He didn't see it as a flaw in a woman and didn't understand how some men did. "So how you doin'?" he added as they shook, their eyes connecting.

"Jeez, Tierney, your mitts are like sandpaper. Must work well for those handjobs."

His gesture was thankfully obscure.

"I'm a farmer now. Raising chickens, planting a garden, going to bed early. If the apocalypse comes, I'm set. Even learned how to make bread. As long as I can defend it, I can stay there forever even if the world goes to hell."

"Until some asshole decides to blow up California."

They shared a hearty chuckle.

An airport traffic police whistled for them to move on, which they both heard and very publicaly ignored. There was still that chip on their shoulders from bar fights and disputes with other dispensers of authority.

A brisk fall wind blew through Garrett's bones. D.C. could be warm this time of year, but today, it was definitely not. Or maybe he was nervous.

"Get in," Branson barked as he rounded to the driver side.

Garrett dropped his duffel into the rear seat and climbed inside a second before Branson gunned the beast and did a two-lane change without signaling.

"I can see you're still working on your reputation, Commander." Branson had crashed his pickup during BUD/S and was nearly rolled back. He'd been stuck with the nickname Crash ever since.

"Haven't had even a ticket since, I'll have you know. Not that I haven't been close."

Garrett stared straight ahead and allowed the

breech of traffic and noise to sink in. He'd forgotten how uncomfortable he was in crowds with too many moving parts. He knew the signs. It was early PTSD. He stared at his hands and they were as steady as granite.

"So where are we headed?"

"Just sit back and relax, Tierney. What we have to say has to be done in controlled space."

Holy hell. What was I thinking?

"So you're DHS now?" he asked.

"Don't you have ears?"

"What? You thinking I'm wearing a wire? With all this activity around us, how could anyone—?"

"Just humor me. We'll be there in a few."

Garrett started to get pissed now. He didn't like this part of government work, the having to be careful about who was listening and what it meant. The not knowing what was behind that smile, the turn of the cheek, or the way someone moved their hands. A stance would trigger him in those days. Now it all came flooding back. He'd underestimated his readiness for this. He should just level with Branson and get back to California.

"You know, Silas, I'm not at all sure I did the right thing coming out here. I've been off the grid for so long, out of the game. I've turned into my mother's hippie dreams. This place doesn't do anything for me except make me want to stop at the bathroom."

Branson gave him a grin and readjusted his military-issue sunglasses. Without looking back at him, he said, "And that's why you're perfect for this job, Garrett. You were the first one I thought of."

So much for secrets.

"In about five minutes, you're gonna have a nice, clean men's room to use, my brother."

It had been a half-hearted try, Garrett realized too late. Now he was sounding like a whiny kid. No one forced him to take that ticket and get on the plane. To wash all his clothes, clean his weapons and go to the target range yesterday and not today so he wouldn't have any residue that security checks would pick up and question him about. He'd checked out all his bills and made sure Snooker had enough food so Geronimo could feed and tend to him while he was away. Those were the things he used to do before deployments. It set off in motion the rest of the things he would need for a mission.

His mind had to be like steel, focused and hard. He had to prune and clip his emotions like he did his beard this morning, being careful not to draw blood when he shaved. He had eyes in the back of his head as he left his driveway, making sure he hadn't attracted someone's special attention. He turned off the auto-answer feature on his home phone, so it would just ring, like he was out in the garden and couldn't come in to answer. Nothing was to look like he would be gone for any length of time. He didn't need to have anyone know he wasn't there to retrieve a message or pay a bill.

In the old days, he didn't hesitate. One step led to the next and the next until he was in full battle gear, sound and ready to react when the time came. Just like he'd been trained. He'd deployed without even knowing what country they'd step out onto when they arrived, so why was this spooking him so much?

He was still the same man. He was ready. He could handle it. He'd seen enough death and dying, blood covering himself and others around him to be ready. He'd held the dying, the men he wanted to save. He'd made love to women trying to excise his demons and only heard the screams of war instead. Intense love-making was a close second, but it didn't dull his memories or the understanding of how fragile life was. He'd tasted the sweet efforts of his home-grown cooking and understood now why he fought so hard. But he fought before he even knew any of that. So why was now so different?

It wasn't.

"You miss those days, Garrett?" Branson asked him as the truck droned on.

"What days? The weddings? The funerals? The—?"

A memory flashed by him. He was holding Connor Lambert in his arms, and although Connor was a big man, it was harder to control his crying than to hold the man's dying body. They shared that look that they'd see each other again, and if it was reversed, Connor would have held him until his last breath was taken. They didn't have to speak; they just looked. It was afterward when the tears and the regrets of not telling him what it was going to feel like missing his best friend began. Nothing came close to that day. Not the day his father was killed in service when Garrett was a boy, not the day his mother gave up her struggle with cancer in the midst of her grief, and not the day his sister went off with some guy she met and never returned. Connor was the only family he'd had. That day would forever be embedded in his psyche.

Damn, Branson!

"I try not to, Si." He wondered if he was too blunt. "I don't miss what we did. We never knew why, so that doesn't figure. I miss the guys, especially the ones who didn't come home."

Branson was quiet, chewing on something, locking his jaws, and then biting his lip. "I hear you. The Boneyard of Bone Frogs. That's a scary place."

He was getting irritated again. "I really didn't come out all this way to talk about that. Most days, I just take what comes."

"Yeah, I know."

They remained silent the rest of the way to the three-story glass office building. The sign out front read *Office of Health, Education and Welfare.* Garrett turned to his buddy. Before he could say anything, Silas interrupted his thoughts.

"Hang in there. I gotta get you passed at the gate. Just be yourself."

Garrett gave him a goofy, cross-eyed grin and drooled.

"Nice."

They drove into a line of cars waiting to clear a sentry station. Garrett thought it was unusual this building would be guarded by a Marine contingent. He signed for the pass that was issued, and he clipped it to the front of his shirt while the young sentry watched carefully. They were shown where to park—in the precise number they were given.

"All will be explained, Tierney. Very soon now."

Garrett noticed the uniforms first. He counted three branches of service represented, including a Navy Vice Admiral, who addressed Branson and frowned at Tierney. He was not given an introduction.

They peeled off into a large room manned by a secretary who logged them in, made note of the information on Garrett's visitor's badge, and then asked him for any electronic devices he was carrying.

He handed her his cell with the cracked screen. She asked them if they wanted water or coffee, and he accepted a cold bottle of water. Then she buzzed them in.

He'd been in controlled rooms before. This one was not as nice as some of the ones he'd been in at the State Department. The long table down the middle was made up of various colors of government-issue grey and tan smaller tables, lined end to end. The chairs were also a mismatch. He saw the computer screen lights peeking behind cabinet doors and knew this could be a war room if the occasion warranted it. A wiped-clean whiteboard was off to the side with two markers in the tray below.

"Sit," Branson commanded.

Garrett did so, unscrewing the top of his water and downing half of it. Branson took a delicate sip from his bottle.

"You need a restroom, first? Sorry. Should have asked you earlier."

"Is this going to take long?" Garrett asked.

"Depends on you, but I don't think so."

"Let's get the party started, then."

"I'm going to just give you a little background. I've been with DHS for about two years now. They recruited me just after—"

"I'm sorry about your boy, Commander."

"No more 'Commander.' Please call me Silas, or Branson. We don't identify as former military unless we're known. Understood?"

"Sure."

"My wife left me, which was the last straw. I wanted to go back to the teams in the worst way, but you know how the Navy is. They got eyes even in the men's room, I think. I'd have to re-qualify, and I had a back injury I'd been covering up. But this injury kept me out." He pointed to his heart.

Garrett felt his blood pressure rise. Branson'd had a string of bad luck. He wondered how he would be able to deal with that double tragedy. It was one of the reasons he wasn't drawn toward the altar himself.

"Look, Branson, I just want to say, I've got huge respect for you and how you've dealt with all this."

"Shut up, Tierney. I didn't bring you all the way out here to get sympathy from you—especially you of all people."

Garrett considered whether he should continue and decided he did, for his own piece of mind. "I just want to say that I'm glad you've found something—"

"Something to believe in again?" The smile on Branson's face seemed brittle.

"Not exactly. But go ahead. I'll shut up." Garrett crossed his arms and leaned back in his chair, determined to keep his mouth shut and keep his emotions clipped.

"We've had some disasters recently, mostly because they hired the wrong men and women for the job. You know how I feel about our brothers on the Teams. That's how I got tasked. They've formed a new division of Homeland Security. We call it Bone Frog Command."

"So everyone dies." Garrett knew that the symbol of the Bone Frog was one of the most sacred symbols of the Teams, equal to the Trident.

"We're pulling guys out of mothballs. Guys who were distinguished SEALs, all Commanders or Lieutenant Commanders. We want men of this caliber to run an inter-departmental team to handle security threats to the homeland. Special projects."

"Mission Impossible? Like the *'Director will disavow any knowledge of you should you fail—'*"

"Everything is a joke to you now, is it? You don't fool me one bit, Tierney. I know you miss the Teams."

Their eyes connected. Garrett knew Branson understood him right down to his toenails.

"You had a rough go with Connor. I remember pulling you out of bars, as did several of your guys. We were relieved when you walked away. You were a danger to yourself and anyone else around you. You were about to blow a decent retirement. I can say this because I was the same way."

He leaned forward and lowered his voice, clasping his hands in front of him. Garrett let him get adjusted.

"This mission is about something so sensitive it cannot go outside this room should you turn me down. And if I thought you'd do that, I wouldn't have asked you to fly out here. We've had some colossal fuckups lately. We're not sure who we can trust here in D.C. We have some internal threats to our way of life. There are even guys in the Head Shed that think the Teams are a bunch of overgrown footballers who can't get it up anymore. Jealousy is ripe. The stench of politics is everywhere.

"And then there's the public, for whom we fought and died. Views have changed. Sometimes the ones we've saved are no longer grateful, not that we did it for that. But it sucks."

"I don't watch the news so all of this doesn't make sense, Si."

"You're a filthy liar, too, Tierney." He grinned, which made Garrett do the same. Branson continued. "The bad guys are here at home. They've always been out there, but our overburdened police, FBI, HS and other departments are overloaded with organized crime and drug enforcement caseloads, stretched so thin they might catch up in the next century. And we want guys most people wouldn't expect would lead a team *inside the United States* to do some special things.

We want guys who get 'er done. In the face of impossible odds."

"Impossible? We never thought anything was impossible."

"Exactly. That's not part of our vocabulary. That's why we want former SEALs. Used to leading a command of misfits from all over the place, welding them into a strong cohesive unit. We need a strike force that goes in, gets the job done, and then fades away into the surf, as the commercial goes. Are you in?"

"Well, it would help if I knew what this impossible feat is."

"Yes, I knew you'd say that. But no can do. So, Garrett Tierney, are you in? You think really long and hard before you answer me because I'm not asking again. And I know I'm asking before you know what the mission is."

Garrett felt the blood rushing to his fingers, which exploded with heat. The pulsing behind his ears sent hissing frequencies to his brain. His gut was empty and wrapping around itself. His balls shrank but his dick was hard. His thighs tensed and wanted to run ten miles or do a hundred pushups. Drips of sweat traveled down the sides of his torso. His breathing was controlled, deep, and his chest full of the excitement of the possibilities being given him.

"Hell yes, I'm in."

CHAPTER 2

MIMI WAGNER EXAMINED the desk three rows back and two rows from the outside wall in her empty classroom. She thought if she concentrated hard enough she could conjure up the face and body of the attractive red-headed girl who used to sit there. Her student Georgette Collier was fond of staring out the window, or dreaming of something while setting her chin on her upturned palm, elbow resting on the desk top. She'd look right at Mimi, but her mind traveled millions of miles away—in some other galaxy.

Georgette enjoyed two things—after boys with good looks and cocky attitudes, that is. She loved science fiction and poetry. Mimi had selected the next series of lessons with Georgette in mind.

Except the young girl wasn't there anymore, and no one revealed when she'd return.

Mimi was used to the cryptic reasons some of her students were pulled out of school. Teaching at Washington Academy, where all the brightest and richest of Washington's special families sent their kids, had not only been a dream job, but a lifesaving event. She loved the interaction, with the young spawn of her country's political and financial elite, as well as the sons and daughters of Ambassadors and captains of industry who would one day be leaders in this or their own countries. But right now, they were kids, kids with raging hormones and all the things that kids did before the crush of responsibility and reputation would grind some of them to a pulp. She'd seen it happen.

But that's why Georgette's absence was so unusual. She shone brightly with a hopelessly romantic view of the world, just like Mimi had been at one time in those golden days before her Navy SEAL father came home in a closed casket.

In her Junior year at the Academy, Georgette had colleges and universities all over the world courting her, and subtlety whispering suggestions to her parents: The president and First Lady of the United States.

If the president or his wife wanted to take Georgette out of school for some special trip or function, who was she to complain? But something about the occurrence didn't sit right with Mimi. The security at the school had been beefed up. There was a flurry of new rules about pickups and deliveries, even for shipments of school supplies. The new classroom observer in didn't dress at all like a teacher. She looked like a well-trained and lethal cop who studied every word she uttered.

Even her friend Carmen didn't speak to Mimi unless in private, as if they were both concerned about being watched.

Something was definitely up.

Her mother had called, inviting her to a weekend in San Diego, even offering to pay for the flight. Mimi guessed she wanted to introduce her to a new potential step-dad. There had been a half-dozen of them in the ten years since her father had come home. She'd stopped visiting the grave site to inform him of the new guy and unload her feelings about how lacking he was compared to her father.

When Mimi was recommended for the exclusive Washington Academy, and got the job, she took it on the spot. Anything to save her from looking out at the ocean and not seeing her father traverse the beach with his surfboard, outrunning most his other Team buddies. Those golden, endless summer days had been the highlight of her life. Now, the challenge of the new school, exclusive student body and interesting international faculty, benefactors and parents kept her mind busy on the here and now.

Those days are gone.

She knew she was strong enough to handle a trip

back to Coronado but just wasn't sure she wanted to. Still, her mother was excited when she agreed.

"*Wonderful! You can have your old room, and—*"

"*That's a no-go, mom. I'm staying at a motel.*"

"*Sure, Mimi. But I thought we could have some girl-time.*"

"*Why don't we rent a house down at the beach at Christmas? Make it a whole week? That would give us more girl-time.*"

"*Well—*"

Even before her mother finished her sentence, Mimi knew the Christmas plans were not going to include her. They were going to include the man she was going to introduce to her, and hopefully get her blessing about before a private Christmas wedding somewhere in Hawaii or the Caribbean.

"*I've sort of got plans for Christmas, and that's why I wanted you to come down this weekend. I can put you up at the Hotel Del—*"

"*Nice. Where Jason and I spent our honeymoon? I'm going to say no to that one.*"

"*Right, I'm sorry. You choose the place, and I'll pay for it.*"

"*How about I pay for everything? I'll fly down Friday night if you can pick me up? I'll try to get a flight not too late?*"

"*Wonderful. We'll be there. Just text me your info.*"

Staring back at Georgette's empty desk, Mimi was struck with the sudden realization that now her other parent was moving on. She knew this day would come eventually. She was glad her mother's long wait was finally over, but that meant she would be sharing her mom with someone new. This turning point meant that indeed Mimi was totally on her own.

You're being too harsh with her said a voice from the ether, as if her Dad was chastising her to quit hanging on. But that's what she was still doing. It totally sucked.

Mimi imagined she could see Georgette's coy little face smiling up at her. How did she deal with an important father who had the weight of the whole country, part of the whole world, on his shoulders? A mother who was rumored to be a handful for the Secret Service detail—but Mimi had only overheard that conversation. It didn't surprise her. Georgette's mother had been a former model, with the sexy eyes that told the world she still missed it.

Everyone moves on. Georgette has "lost" both her parents, like I have.

On the day they came to the door to speak with her mother about her father's demise, she'd seen the fear smeared all over the face of the female Chaplain in the notification detail. Mimi had wondered how this woman could go on with her life after visiting dozens of sad families like she did that day. Did she go home and hug her children to reassure them she was still among the living or to reassure herself that she wasn't affected?

Mimi's rock that day had been her father's best friend, Garrett Tierney, who grabbed her tight and held her fourteen-year-old body so intensely she felt the hug for days afterward. She could still today smell the odor of him, the sweat from the long plane ride. He told the story of how her father had died. He held her mother, who had to be given something and was brought to the bedroom by a nurse the Navy had sent along.

That left her staring back at Tierney—the man who was always second, behind her father. He was a better fish, her dad used to say, and a much better womanizer, much to her mother's relief. She and her mother had loved hearing about the pair's exploits, her father's handsome face lighting up when he told them of some of the pranks they used to pull on each other.

She had wanted to be brave that day after her mother was taken to the bedroom, but her lower lip began to quiver. Then he was there, kneeling in front of her, pulling her to him, and breathing words into her ear she wished she could now remember. She was consumed with him. She wanted to ask him if he could stay, even though she missed and would forever miss her dad. He felt and smelt so much like her Dad. She wasn't ready to let go. Why couldn't they just let Garrett Tierney stay for a day until she'd cried all her tears away, until her mother could get up out of bed?

That had been ten years ago last month, the anniversary not even planned with a special gravesite visit or family gettogether or a phone call. It just drifted off like any other day. She was in D.C., and her mother was still in Southern California. They both had moved on as best they could.

Suddenly, the doors to her classroom opened, sending a brisk hallway breeze forward, accentuating the tear that had developed under Mimi's right eye. She quickly wiped it away with the back of her hand and stood to meet her visitors.

Two young men and a woman entered the classroom. She didn't recognize any of them, but from their appearance, she took them for FBI, Homeland Security, or Secret Service detail. If they were Capitol Police, they'd be in uniform, since this was not a social call. She instantly had an inkling it was going to have something to do with Georgette's absence.

"Mrs. Wagner?" one of the men asked her. He appeared to be about the same age as she was, around twenty-eight.

"That's me. What can I do for you?" She rounded the desk and extended her hand.

"I'm Special Agent Peter Hoaglund. This is Special

Agent Ron Desideri."

Mimi gave them a firm handshake that was returned. Desideri was wearing too much cologne.

She next turned to the stunningly attractive woman a step behind, who had been studying the introductions. She was about the same age as her own mother. Peter Hoaglund cleared his throat and began.

"This is Felicia Menendez. She's with the State Department," he said, his voice breaking like a youth.

"I've heard glowing things about you, Mimi," Felicia boomed. "Glad we get to meet." She gripped Mimi's hand and shook it furiously.

In the presence of such beauty and feminine confidence, Mimi felt self-conscious of her plain attire designed to downplay some of her curves. The woman from State was dressed in a midnight blue tailored suit, accentuating her slim waist and thighs as well as her doe-like ankles atop four-inch shiny navy-blue heels. Her blonde hair was dark at the roots and spun into an attractive French twist, with shaggy bangs framing her pale pink face. She polished off the look with bright red lipstick. Her hair and face were the only parts of her that appeared out of control, but everything else was stealth, muscled and perhaps dangerous. Even her squinting smile made Mimi's pulse race, as if Ms. Menendez didn't want to waste a crease in her otherwise flawless face. As a mature woman, she was hotter than D.C. summers in July. Mimi noticed she made the men nervous.

The woman was a predator.

"Thanks. I'm sure my students don't share the enthusiasm, but I'll take the compliment anyway. So what brings you to room 402?"

Hoaglund suggested they sit, so several of the desks were moved into a fan shape—the three of them arched and facing Mimi's single desk like it was a firing squad. Now she knew for certain this had something to do with Georgette.

While Ms. Menendez scanned every square inch of the classroom walls, acting uninterested in the conversation, Hoaglund began the discussion.

"We're here about the president's daughter, Georgette. I'm not sure what you've been told—but—"

"Yes, what *have* you been told, my dear?" Ms. Menendez asked like a hot knife through soft butter, her focus unwavering. Hoaglund was noticeably surprised but didn't interrupt the exchange.

"Well, just that she wouldn't be in for a while. It was very vague. Usually, I get notice, at least a week or two, but in this case, she just didn't show up that next day, and I was told mid-morning she wouldn't be attending for some time. Something about a last-minute trip."

"Who told you it was a last-minute trip?" Ms.

Menendez asked, her voice rushed and holding a twinge of irritation.

"My principal, Dr. Andrews. That was a week ago now."

Menendez turned to Hoaglund on her left. "Why wasn't she interviewed immediately?"

Before the Special Agent could answer, Mimi answered. "I was. Someone from the White House came to get her assignments, and asked me questions about Georgette, her studies, and how she'd been doing. If there was any particular part of her school work she was having trouble with, that sort of thing."

"She should have had a formal interview, not just surveillance," replied Agent Desideri. The two others nodded their heads.

"Surveillance?" Acid was brewing in the pit of her stomach.

The pause was painful. She looked between the faces of all three of the representatives, and Mimi knew she wasn't going to like what they told her next.

"We have a situation here. The Department wanted to work out all the details before we made our plans known. But, Mrs. Wagner, Georgette Collier is missing, and we're assembling a team to help get her back." Agent Hoaglund's face was icy cold and white with fear.

"Missing? You mean kidnapped?"

"Maybe. That's what we're trying to determine. She may have left of her own accord, and then met up with undesirables. We need to keep this quiet, and we're only telling those people who are involved in the plan to find her."

"So why are you telling me, then?"

The three of the visitors didn't smile as they watched her begin to understand what they'd come for.

CHAPTER 3

"**S**O, GARRETT, WE'RE going to be joined in a few by some VIPs," Commander Branson said as he returned from the outside office, checking his backwards-strapped analog watch. He slapped some brown folders down on the table. "I've got about an hour to go over what I know and give you an update, and then we'll get further instructions from the surveillance team."

"Surveillance?"

"Yes. This is about Georgette Collier. We call her Sorrel, and she's missing."

"The president's daughter?"

"The very one. We've managed to keep the press out of it, so far. But that is likely to change. That's why you haven't heard it before."

"Makes no difference to me. I don't watch the news," Garrett announced. His mind devised the questions he needed answered quickly, already working out a template of a plan, and who he would need on his team.

"She took off sometime between the end of school on the fifth and the morning of the sixth. Her detail was to take her home. It's a gated, private Academy—"

"Washington Academy?"

"Affirmative."

"I know how it works. So how did she manage to get out?"

"We're going to get that briefing when the others arrive."

"This your op?"

"No, Tierney, this is one hundred percent yours. And that's what I have to talk to you about. You're our first for this new Bone Frog Command. I can't tell you how much is riding on your shoulders. If this goes bad, our whole command could be S O L."

"Fuck, Comman—Branson. You had to start with me?"

"No, actually, we were going to start with another type of mission, but this came up. They'd been working on this team for awhile. Then they drew me in, and when this happened, I told them I had the man for the job already and that there was no reason to delay."

"So she's been gone a week."

"Nearly. We were doing very low-profile checks, double checking her detail, looking for someone or something out of the ordinary. We discussed her home patterns with the White House staff. But it's like she just created this departure all by herself, just discovered a hole in her protection team, used it, and got out."

Garrett knew the young girl probably saw it as breaking free from prison, with the weight of the public eye on her constantly. And her decisions hadn't caused it. Her parents' had. He knew it would be a grinder for a young kid, especially a young girl.

"You going to be advisor on this, though?"

"You report to me. But it's your gig. And in case you're thinking about it, this isn't something you can say no to. I told them to come on over, so no backing out."

"No worries there. I said I wanted in. I meant it. I'm just trying to figure out who we're going to need. The most obvious thing we need is someone who knows her well. Like very well. She have a confidante?"

"We're working on that. She's been a handful for her parents and the White House domestic staff. She flirts with anyone she can get away with, and we've had some transfers because of it. Nothing has happened as far as we can tell. She's allowed a computer but with some very strict procedures she appeared to be follow-ing. She's just a teen. Sixteen years old. Boy crazy. She's got friends, but she likes the boys. For all we can tell, she thinks this is just some great lark."

"Jeez. The president must be beside himself."

"He is. So is the First Lady. She's a ball-buster."

"Oh, I get it. I remember an assignment over in Africa when she was visiting villages there right in the middle of a military coup. Freaked all of us out. She pulled the same thing on us. I'm guessing she's told that story to her daughter."

"Unfortunately, it fits the pattern. So you see what we're up against? These people want to live a normal life—doing crazy stuff, on occasion—and we're supposed to keep them safe. If there's any loss of life, it's supposed to be us, not them, that pays. But anyone who works around the State Department or the White House understands this and has to be okay with it. Like sending a bunch of incredibly well-trained young men into a hellhole and expecting them to pull off something a whole Marine division couldn't accomplish, without harming any innocents. But we did it, didn't we, Tierney? We were those guys"

"We were." Garrett indulged in the pride he had for his brothers and the SEAL community, who were generally quiet, did what it took at whatever cost, most times without much of a thank you and no knowledge from the general public. This was the same thing.

"You ever meet them?"

"Met her in Africa, once, as I said. He was a Senator back when I met President Green at Connor's service."

He chuckled.

"I fail to feel the joke here, Tierney."

"Man, the instructions I was given to tell to my little platoon before the service read something like what Admiral Nelson had tried to instill on his troops in Antigua. Something having to do with if they let their eyes roam, they'd all go blind with a pencil stuck in their eye sockets."

Branson cracked a smile too.

"Sorry, Si. You know how those things just pop into your head at the wrong times."

"I do. And the Mrs. is hard not to stare at. I get it. She likes it that way."

Garrett shook his head. "She sure does."

After a brief pause, Branson steered them back to the mission at hand. "We okay here, Tierney? With Connor's death? Understand it was one of the reasons you left the Teams."

"We are. It's past history. All my boys were focused on the send-off, on the widow and the kid. They loved Connor—"

Garrett breathed in several times before he could continue. He was back in control now.

"Connor was one of those guys who was legendary, you know? After that, and even after my promotion and distance from the active theater, I still couldn't imagine doing anything without him. We were each other's backup."

Branson leaned forward. "I sure as hell remember that. Everyone who knew him thought the same."

"So, let's talk about the structure. I get to pick who I want?"

"With approval, yes."

"Whose approval?"

"Mine. Unless something begins to go sideways, or they hear something they don't like. You're going to be watched, Tierney. And there will be some who get an inkling but are not in the loop, and they'll be jealous. You know how these things go."

"Don't remind me. It's where all our fuckups came from. Politics."

"Exactly. So, as long as you and I stay tight, and we're completely honest with each other, every aspect of the mission will be directed and controlled by you, until you prove you can't handle it. If this one goes well, you'll be finding some good employment for some other former Commanders who are being considered for new missions coming up. Might even be a place for you in the future here, running these teams. But no promises. This is a one-off. So, you fuck it up for you, you fuck it up for several others of our brothers. That won't make me happy."

"I won't be military, then? I'll be DHS?"

"Yeah. If you're lucky, you get to double dip."

"Like that's important."

"I knew that too. So, Garrett, let's go over some deets. I'm sure you got a ton of questions. Write them down here."

Branson shoved a white-ruled notepad across the table and tossed him a pen.

Garrett began to draw a grid. "Okay, so we need to know what she was doing the few days before she disappeared. Who was the last to see her?"

"As far as we know, her teacher."

"I'm sure you've inspected the videos at the school?"

"She doesn't show up on any of them after she left class. That's the funny part."

"She must have had help. The teacher?"

"No, I don't think so. In fact, we're going to have her on the team. She's been briefed this morning, too."

"Don't trust her, yet, but I'll play along. Not sure I want a female on my team."

"You said you wanted a confidante."

"Yeah, someone who stays at home and keeps her mouth shut."

Branson leaned back and crossed his arms. "You never got married, did you, Tierney."

"Nope."

"Why doesn't that surprise me?"

"This is a mission. This is real life. Marriage? That's a fantasy." He believed every word he uttered. Marriage was a fairy tale mothers told their daughters. Garrett believed marriage had no place for a man of action. There was only one master, and that was his Team, to his brothers, to the mission at hand. Everything else was expendable. He didn't want to get an innocent involved, someone with soft feelings. It made things more dangerous.

"Look at me, Tierney. I still believe in love. I also believe in second chances. Nothing can't be fixed if you got enough grit and love and some of that 'don't quit' attitude we were trained for. Some stresses can't be overcome by everyone. No harm, no foul. My wife had to get out of the pot before she melted. It was the right thing to do at the time. Didn't make it easy, but it was something I'm glad she did now. We'd have been miserable the rest of our lives if she'd kept everything inside, 'shut up' as you say, and tried to stick it out."

"And now?"

Branson grinned. "I got her back. Even have a little one on the way. Got remarried several months ago now."

Garrett was envious. But there wasn't anyone in his past he regretted losing, except Connor. No woman had cracked that outer shell, and never would.

"Well, there's a big star for you, then. I suppose that makes you the better man."

Branson started to interrupt him, but Garrett held

him off with a show of his enormous palm.

"I don't have anyone and never really did. I like to fly solo, unless I have a partner like Connor, and that's not going to happen again, so we'll just have to disagree on that score. Congrats and all that, but now, let's get back to some other details."

Silas was silent, watching Garrett design his basic grid perimeter, listing the unknowns and the knowns, adding the cast of characters, assessing where their weaknesses would be, and trying to select people who might fill that hole. He hadn't come to the part about fixing the confidante hole when there came a knock at the door.

He hadn't met the two men he pegged as Special Agents, who entered first and then introduced themselves. They were probably either agents for the Secret Service or State, because they looked too young to be FBI. He had a couple choices for team slots with two or three of his Bureau friends who were considering retirement, but these two, hardly old enough to shave, must be information gatherers, strictly background, and at the beginning of their careers. Probably a temporary assignment so they could prove themselves.

Behind them stood two women, not one. He knew the first one, knew quite a few things about her—like how she liked to be handcuffed when she fucked, how she loved being creative in bed and tried to be dominant, something he found fascinating, but never liked. Their night-long tussles were more akin to an athletic competition.

He was trying to figure out how the former Deputy Ambassador to Nigeria would become a school teacher, until he saw the non-descript Rubinesque woman standing behind her wearing horn-rimmed glasses that nearly covered her face.

"Morning, Garrett. It's been too long," Felicia said in that hoarse, commanding tone that still made his hair stand on end. The two youngsters shared a look between them but kept quiet.

Silas Branson rose. "Well, I didn't realize we knew each other. I wasn't told—"

Felicia Menendez interrupted him without apology. "Commander Branson, Garrett and I go way back." Her eyes hooked into Garrett's and wouldn't allow him to pull away. He wasn't going to let her see his fear level rise.

"And," she said, focusing now on Branson, "the First Lady herself asked me to come along for the interviews, and some of the background. I've known this girl even before she was born." She scanned the circle of characters, stopping to study Garrett.

"Okay," Hoaglund announced separating the air so everyone could breathe. "This is Mrs. Mimi Wagner, who was Georgette's teacher at the Academy."

Mrs. Wagner was clearly outmatched as far as rank. Garrett noticed she would have very kind eyes if she wasn't scared to death like she was now. Her cheeks were soft and rosy, and her clothes didn't cover up her ample chest. He regretted telling Branson she couldn't be trusted. He knew instantly she could be, because he didn't pick up an ounce of rancor or evil. He decided to reach out to her and ignore Felicia Menendez.

"Sorry to drag you into this, Mrs. Wagner," he said as he extended his hand. She barely touched him past his first knuckles in the weakest handshake he'd ever received, even for a woman.

The young teacher looked shocked, stumbling on her words, saying something and then faltering. Garrett couldn't make out anything she was trying to communicate.

Agent Desideri, about the same age as the young teacher, spoke up, coming to her aid. "Mrs. Wagner is probably much more comfortable with Poetry and English Grammar, aren't you, ma'am?"

Garrett wondered why she didn't take her eyes off him, but merely nodded, as if she was in some kind of trance. He saw her fear and didn't want to have that permeate the room.

"Well, let's take our seats, because I have some questions," he barked.

Branson added his comments as he grabbed his

chair. "Let me just start out by laying down the ground rules a bit. We don't address anyone in military terms, so Commander Tierney and Commander Branson are just Garrett and Si. He has full discretion on who he wants as part of the team. This is an informational meeting. No one here should assume they are part of the task force until we hear it from Garrett. And just so you know, Ms. Menendez—"

"That's Deputy Ambassador Menendez, please," she said pertly.

"Well, Ms. Menendez, there aren't going to be any more surprises coming from the White House, with all due respect. We sometimes get mixed messages coming from the family, but mostly from the staff. It's essential that we make sure Garrett is fully in command. Understood?"

She gave Branson a sexy wide grin, and, with a slight nod of her forehead, said, "I like it when a man of action is in charge. I think it bodes well for the outcome." She looked directly at Garrett.

Holy cow. If there ever was a more fucked beginning to a high-level operation, he couldn't remember it. Garrett had two females he hadn't chosen. Neither of them was equipped with anything they'd need on a mission of this type. The Special Agents needed to see real blood and real death, not make-believe things they'd studied in school. This wasn't Disneyland.

Silas Branson had been sideswiped on his first assignment by the White House, and not by the man himself but his wife, the most difficult woman in the entire world, if he believed the stories told about her. And here was her best friend, the woman Garrett had saved from the embassy bombing shortly before he got out, the one who helped him see a portion of himself so disgusting he knew he'd never want to be in a committed relationship. And he'd fucked her. Dozens of times.

If it wasn't totally against his Creed and Code of Conduct, he'd almost started thinking of himself as a victim.

He was going to have to take charge before they all got demoted or killed.

CHAPTER 4

O NE OF MIMI'S complaints about the Academy was how slow things took to get approved, planned and executed. But today, they were moving at light speed. When the two Agents brought her back to her classroom, she was told by her waiting principal that a sub had already been arranged for tomorrow and the days, perhaps weeks, to follow. The story was going to be she had a family emergency involving her mother. He'd known about Georgette from the beginning.

She was also told she had two hours to pack.

"Pack? For what?" she asked as she and Agent Desideri walked to the school parking lot. Hoaglund joined them a few seconds later.

"Taking the Team to a safe location. We've rented a house an hour away."

"What do I pack?"

"Like for a vacation, camping trip. Clothes you'd wear going to visit your mom," Agent Desideri said, wiggling his sizeable curly eyebrows. He shrugged at Mimi's shocked reaction.

"No one ever told me about all this," she whispered as they ushered her toward her car.

"Keys?" Hoaglund held out his hand.

"I can drive just fine."

"I gotta have the keys, Mrs. Wagner."

Mimi churned in her purse and handed the tall blonde young man her fistful of keys. She and Desideri led the way with Hoaglund following behind in her car, until they reached her apartment some ten minutes away from school.

Her heartbeat was so strong her hands were shaking. She'd barely been introduced to Commander Tierney, and now everything she'd been living the past year was being shoved to the back room as if she was running from the law. Was he going to the same location? And why didn't they ask her permission for the "witness protection" detail she was being put under?

She found it difficult to think or make choices. In her haste, she'd picked out six tops and one pair of pants, so she dumped the contents on her bed for the third time and neatly folded everything back. Taking inventory of her underwear and socks, always things she forgot to bring, she also added two more pairs of jeans, her stretchy, comfortable ones. And a bathing suit, which she would most definitely take if she were going to San Diego. But Virginia? She didn't even know all the freeways an hour out of D.C. yet. It was like being taken to some secret encampment.

At the last minute she threw in her tattered back-pack she'd used all throughout college. It was her good luck charm.

The boys carried the bags downstairs for her. She brought her computer case and two jackets then grabbed her cosmetic bag just before closing the door on her old life. Having decent face paint was necessary. If it was going to mean a new chapter in her life, at least she'd look good running through it.

She had lots of questions as they drove out of the city. The biggest one nagging on her was if, when, and who she should tell her story to? Obviously, no one had put together the dots, or realized that her father and this SEAL Commander she was supposed to partner with had been best buddies. Hardest of all was trying to speak, around him, look at him, or stand next to him and have that familiar manly scent make her brain go fuzzy. She was hoping he didn't recognize or remember her, not that he did and was being an efficient asshole. She wasn't about to let go of her fantasies about the man unless she had to. The jury was still out on that one.

Suddenly, Mimi remembered her tentative agreement with her mother for the visit to San Diego.

"I have to call my mother, or she'll be expecting me this weekend. I'm not going to be anywhere close to San Diego."

"I'd say that's a no-brainer, Mrs. Wagner."

She dialed her mother, who picked up on the first ring. Soft music was in the background and Mimi guessed her soon-to-be stepfather was lurking around somewhere close.

"Hey sweetie! Got it all arranged?"

"No, Mom. Listen, I've been called out for a school field trip I can't get out of. One of the other teachers is home with the flu and I'm the next on the list. I tried to get out of it." She peered across the seat at agent Desideri, who rose his eyebrows.

"Oh darn. We were making some nice plans. Where will you be?"

"Somewhere in the Virginia woods, Mom." She again searched agent Desideri's smiling face. He nodded his approval. She knew that would be the extent of what she could tell her. "I'll call when I'm back in town."

"Stay out of the poison ivy and watch for those mosquitos and deer ticks with Lyme disease and all that going on."

"No worries."

Mimi signed off and then leaned back in the seat,

placing her fingers to her forehead, feeling the beginnings of a headache.

"That was easy," Agent Hoaglund said from the back seat.

"Yes, my mother would have a heart attack if she knew what I was really up to. She thinks my biggest worry are ticks and mosquitos—oh, and poison ivy."

"I've had to tell girlfriends some mighty crazy stories. After awhile, they stopped believing me completely. It was better that way," added Desideri.

She smiled at the young agent and didn't see how he possibly could be old enough to have experiences he couldn't reveal to a girlfriend.

They had left the busy, over-taxed grid of D.C. and wound through two-lane roads bordered by trees turning colors in bright orange and yellows. It would have been a beautiful, crisp fall day if it was a real vacation. But nothing about this afternoon was real.

"So will I be under house arrest or something?"

Desideri had a chuckle over that. "Who do you think we are?"

"I have no idea. What do I tell my mom if she calls?"

"Tell her you're chasing a missing kid." Desideri turned and faced her. "It's sort of the truth."

"If she gets any inkling, she'll be all over my case."

"Ask Tierney, if you've got questions what to say.

He'll have a solution."

"So, he's the boss of me right now?" She couldn't help thinking she sounded like one of her students.

Desideri gave her a warm smile, then checked his rearview mirror to make contact with Hoaglund sitting behind him, and answered, "Pretty much. But you're in good hands. He's a highly decorated former Navy SEAL Commander. He was specially picked for this mission."

"So is he going out to the house too? Or, does he get to keep his own place in D.C.?"

"Commander Tierney will be joining you. I believe he lives in California."

"You and Hoaglund?"

"We live in Maryland."

"No, I meant, are you guys staying out at this mysterious hangout?"

"We'll be back and forth. We're responsible for logistics now. Getting you guys situated, procuring food, equipment, things Garrett and the team thinks they'll need. Basically, we're errand-boys. We're working on some things right now."

"I would hope so. Why the delay?"

"What do you mean? We've been working on this twenty-four seven," he asked.

"So you were working behind the scenes? Why all of a sudden do you have Commander Tierney involved? And why me?"

"This is a new command, just created and Tierney is the first guy hired to set up his own team. And while this was being greenlighted, we were working with the White House staff, watching for someone to make a move that would flag they were responsible for her disappearance."

"What kind of move?"

"A ransom demand or something. We've been tracking and studying everyone around her." He turned to face her briefly. "Yes, we've been watching you too."

"Great."

"Well, you asked."

She kept her arms folded across her chest, biting her lower lip. It sucked.

"Trust me, we've been busy, but nothing's come up. No communications of any kind, and no one acting like they're involved. It's like she just disappeared without a trace."

Mimi knew there was no real way anyone could just totally drop out of sight. But then, she'd never tried.

She remembered the electricity between Commander Tierney and the Deputy Ambassador.

"Is the Ambassador part of the team?"

"Only if Tierney wants her." He chuckled. "From

the looks of things, I'm thinking no."

"So, she won't be staying with us?"

"No, ma'am. Tierney will be adding to the team, but right now, you're it."

Oh great.

But then, she caught herself. The vision of Georgette Collier, perhaps all alone, maybe lost, kidnapped, or confused, regretting being pulled away from the safety of the Secret Service detail, no matter how obnoxious it might feel, and knowing she could be scared—that thought changed everything for Mimi. By now, did Georgette understand what kind of danger she was in? And did she do it? Or was it forced upon her?

They pulled through an open iron gate, driving down a gravel path which arched to the right until a large home came into view. Leaves whirled to the sides as the car plowed through the covered drive. The place must have been eight or nine bedrooms with grounds that used to be well manicured and still had the bones of something stately.

"Holy cow. Who owns this place?"

"Drug seizure. Uncle Sam is the proud owner. One of the nice percs of having those confiscation laws."

A four-door grey Suburban was parked in front.

"That must be Tierney's rental," murmured Hoaglund. "Let's see who he dragged along."

Mimi scowled, got out and began to handle her

bags.

"Leave them. Go on inside. We'll bring them in for you."

"Which means you're going to go through them, aren't you?"

"You know how important this op is, Mrs. Wagner. We don't leave anything to chance. But for your information, Tierney himself requested we do so. He doesn't want any weapons or pot or pills entering the home, anything he doesn't know about."

"Great. When is the strip search?"

She could see that annoyed Desideri, who had taken her attitude with some humor, but now the humor left his face, and he yanked her overnight bag from her as he barked to her face. "She's the fuckin' daughter of the president and First Lady of the United States. I'd say this is a little more important than chaperoning a school field trip. The sooner you take this seriously, the faster we can start to get some real progress going."

He was right, of course, but Mimi was trying to get over Garrett Tierney, her father's former best friend, having ordered her things be searched. Maybe she should tell him after all. Tonight. When it was just the two of them. Maybe they'd dump her from the team. Now she wished she'd tossed her vibrator into the suitcase.

"What's so funny?" agent Desideri asked.

"None of your business. That's a need to know for me, and very private." She worked hard to stop from bursting out laughing.

She'd always dreamt about the day she'd get to meet Tierney again, she just didn't think they'd be alone in a house in the woods somewhere.

Careful what you wish for.

She dropped her arms and allowed Desideri to take the bag from her. She twirled on her toes and headed for the house—where her future, whatever that was— lay in front of her. The mission her father had been on had taken him away from her forever. Her Navy SEAL husband was killed in a training accident before he could deploy. Was this mission now going to take her fantasy life away forever too?

Mimi opened the large carved doors that lumbered on squeaky hinges that needed oil. And there he was, poring over papers, just like her father had done years ago. He had a long-necked opened bottle of beer to the side. The light was dim, except for the reflection off the glass coffee table onto his face. His light blue shirt was the same color as his blue eyes.

She'd dreamt of this reunion in a hundred different ways. But when he looked up at her, all of them faded into the ether. What was the same was the way her heart thumped in her chest, the her neck tingled, her fingers pulsed, and her eyes filled with tears.

Yes, she was scared. But it didn't have anything to do with the mission.

CHAPTER 5

"**H**EY THERE, MRS. Wagner." He stood, looking for the agents who were supposed to bring her. "Where are the Cub Scouts?"

"They're bringing in my things. Going through them, first, just like you asked."

She raised her chin to accept his reaction. Her defiant stare signaled he'd been right about the strength of her emotional sinew. She was measured, unwilling to take wild leaps, and he knew this mission wasn't anything she ever thought she'd be involved in.

Makes two of us.

"It's protocol," he tried to say casually, but the truth was, she made his pulse thump. She didn't deserve to be handled roughly. He knew plenty of women who liked it that way, but she was definitely not one of them. He needed to be careful or slip her off the team quietly, for her own safety. That would cause a shit-storm with the White House. Last thing he needed was an altercation with the First Lady or her best friend. He wanted to keep both women as far away as possible. So for now, Mimi Wagner stayed. Besides, from what he'd read, she'd already been through a lot with the loss of her husband.

"Look, Mrs. Wagner—"

"If I'm not to call you anything but Garrett, I guess you should call me Mimi."

"Duly noted, Mimi. I do it out of deference to your husband, an old habit. I just read this morning that—"

"About a year ago, thank you. But I'm fine. I *get* the body language and the lingo. Although, my husband wasn't like any SEAL I'd ever met before. And I've met a few."

She was studying him closely, and that put him on alert. "Still, I'm sorry for your loss."

"Thank you."

The young agents burst through the doorway. "Where do you want these, Commander?"

"I've just been reminded we're to stop doing that. So, stop it, or I'll get you on someone else's detail." He settled his breathing then fisted and unfisted his hands while he waited for them to realize the blunder they'd made. He'd left them speechless, so he started in patiently.

"If everything's okay, you can put those upstairs in the bedroom with the flowered wallpaper."

He thought he'd get a rise out of Mimi if he followed that comment by wiggling his eyebrows, and he wasn't disappointed. The two agents tore up the stairs, rattling the windows, as if they were ten years old and it was a race to get to the toys.

"Thank God they didn't find my Glock, and I don't have the nursery," she answered. Her mouth was twisted. He could see she was having a hard controlling a budding grin.

Good for you. You play nice, but you are firm. And you have a sense of humor. I like that. And I'll watch how I behave.

"I hope you're kidding, but should I search you?" The thought thrilled him.

At first, with her look of panic and her eyes growing nearly the size of her glasses made him think perhaps he'd run into someone who had a phobia about men touching her. That would be just his luck. She was hard to figure out.

"Okay, now I'm kidding," he reassured her.

One of the things he noted after he directed her to sit across from him was the way she moved and the size of her bust, along with the incredible way she smelled. A woman's flowery, feminine smell—that combination of face cream, shampoo, and perfume—he always found disarming.

Most women thought they had to show cleavage or

good legs or heavy shadow on their eyes—which made them look, at least to Garrett, more Goth or drugged up than anything else. There was nothing more alluring than the woman's flowing clothes, layering and pressing around her hips, her waist, and pulling up at all the right places with a tease she had no idea she was tempting him with. He also liked that she didn't look threadbare, have that hard-and-often-ridden look of a dangerous, uncontrollable woman.

Damn, he was getting turned on at a very inconvenient time. He decided he needed to open the door to understanding her, her background, and what she was all about. And he had the right, as well as the desire, to do it too.

"So, Mimi," he said with a bow-like gesture as he sat, "your Academy file is sorely missing lots of detail." He examined a file in front of him. "You're a widow and married a SEAL who was training to deploy. So, you know a lot about our community, as you've said."

"Yes."

Her eyes bored into him. He thought he caught a sparkle in one corner, as if something had made her tear up.

"I know this type of discussion can be hard, but we've got to get to know each other well if we're going to work together. It needs to be almost symbiotic. If you're uncomfortable with that, you need to let me know."

"Being honest?"

"Yes, be totally honest with me."

The boys came downstairs. Garrett handed them some money from his pocket and a list.

"There's a store about two miles north. You passed it. I think you can get everything there."

"When will the others be arriving?" Desideri asked.

"Undetermined and not appropriate to ask yet. So, get on your way." As an afterthought, he added, "And don't forget the receipt, gentlemen."

They both darted for the door. Desideri paused to ask a question of Mimi. "Ma'am, do you need anything special at the store?"

"I'm fine. Maybe some waters?"

"Plain, mineral? Fancy?"

"Plain is fine."

"You got it."

They slammed the door behind them, which left the cold interior of the huge house and just the two of them to fill it. Knowledge, understanding, and cooperation would be best. But anything to eliminate the vacuum.

He crossed and uncrossed his legs, picked up the lined tablet Branson had given him. "Now you were about to be honest with me. Tell me about yourself. They'll be providing me with a file, but I'd like to hear about you with your own words first."

She ran her fingers through her mahogany hair, which was long but curly, held with a clip she removed and then replaced. He liked the look of it long during those brief seconds and decided not to hold back on the smile to show her so.

She was scowling when she removed her large, oval glasses and wiped them on the edge of her skirt between her thumb and third finger. She looked out the large dining room window into the woods, deep in thought. The silent view the trees resembled large overstretched ghostly shadows. Dusk was upon them. It felt like the witching hour.

She angled her head, holding her glasses in her right hand, and then peered across the coffee table at him, leaning forward. Her eyes looked familiar, but he knew he'd have remembered her if they'd ever dated. Mimi was a diamond in the rough, a beautiful, unspoiled specimen of feminine strength. When he was younger, she would be just his type. Her face was peachy and fresh, and he had the overwhelming desire to kiss her. If this was a date, he'd have done it by now. But this was no date.

"You don't remember me, do you?" she whispered, then put back her glasses, blinking as she did so.

Garrett suddenly felt himself turn red. Something inside him had blown up. Had he slept with her before?

He was sure he'd have remembered. His confidence oozed right out of the bottoms of his shoes.

"I'm sorry. I don't believe we've met. Correct me, if I'm wrong. And, if so, I'm very, very sorry."

"You have nothing to feel sorry about. I told you I knew a lot about Navy SEALs. As it turns out, you knew my dad."

Panic started to constrict Garrett's chest. Had he been hitting—okay, not hitting, but *thinking about hitting*—on the daughter of a buddy? Holy smoke. Talk about going from bad to worse!

"Who is your dad?"

"Connor Lambert."

He shot up, screaming, "No! You're the—the—daughter."

"Margaret. Yes, Dad used to call me Maggie. I decided to leave that for him and changed my name to Mimi afterwards. But I'm Margaret Lambert."

Garrett stared down at her like she was an injured dog he needed to treat. He'd violated her already with his stupid, disgusting behavior.

"Maggie—Margaret, sorry, Mimi. I'll honor that. Look at you!" He didn't know what else to say. It wasn't appropriate to tell her she'd grown up a stunner, that with her braids and braces gone, she was a thoroughly mature, attractive young woman. And the spitting image of his best friend, Connor. That's when he realized those eyes of hers that he thought he recognized were indeed the eyes of that fourteen-year-old girl who'd just lost her father. The young, fragile girl he'd held in his arms and wished he could give some comfort. He'd thought about her and her mother and wondered what had become of them. He'd heard rumors of her mom. But he'd always wanted to know how they fared. He'd been too removed to know about Mimi's husband.

He came around the coffee table and held his arms wide, not wanting to step on anything that smacked of something inappropriate. He was asking for permission to give her a hug.

She stood and stepped carefully to him, leaning against his chest with her head staring down at her feet. That's when his arms encircled her, hugging her tight against him, his hands holding her head tenderly. "God, I'm so sorry I didn't know."

The two of them swayed together for several seconds. He felt like he'd captured a big, beautiful but wounded exotic creature. It had been a long time since he'd shared any of his private grief with anyone else who felt the same way.

But now, what about the mission?

He separated them at arm's length, gripping the top of her arms.

"You can't be here. They should have—"

"Garrett," she said as she stepped back two paces and found a safe space to stand. "I'm the only one I think she'll listen to. I don't care what that—that woman has to say, Georgette's not close with her parents, especially her mother. Anything that comes from them, won't be trusted. But if something's happened to her, I can identify her. I can identify her out of a crowd, in a hospital, in disguise, or—God forbid—in a morgue. I can tell if it's her on the phone, or if her text message is legit. I don't think even her mother could do that."

She was right, but the added burden of their shared grief and past, made this a very bad idea, Garrett realized.

"I just don't know. We'll have to tell them, Branson and the president, of course."

"Of course. If they want me off the team, so be it. It's your call. No hard feelings either way if the answer is I go back to teaching. This isn't what I do. It's what *you* do, Garrett. If it was my dad standing here before me I'd say the same thing. You gotta do what you gotta do for the Team, like always. If I'm in the way, I go home."

Garrett wanted to reassure her—but he wasn't positive he could trust his feelings yet. After all, the decision could be out of his control, despite what they'd told him.

Mimi began to pace the floor, turning here and there to add emphasis to her thoughts. He followed every movement she made like he was her student.

"Meanwhile, instead of talking about me, why don't we talk about you, Garrett? If that's too personal, we can talk about Georgette. I can tell you everything I know about her. I'm here to help. This isn't a camping trip, like one of your boys reminded me. There's a lot at stake."

He liked how she thought. She had the same calm logic that he'd relied on with Conor at his side. He knew she was concerned for Georgette, and this was definitely not an arena she was comfortable in, but she was able to work through those emotions and get to the point.

God, how he loved women who could just get right to it.

Keep it straight and narrow.

"Go for it, Mimi. I'm listening."

"I don't know how your normally do things, Garrett. And maybe I don't fit in, or get to stay, but I'm here to help however I can. I'd like to see her back safe and sound. There are a lot of things that could happen to her, and I've read enough books to imagine hundreds of ways this could end. Most of them are not very happy."

She definitely was an asset. He decided to stop

fighting himself, and start using what she had to offer. She was completely right.

"Can I ask you a question first?" he asked.

"Of course." She gave him a timid smile.

"When did you know?"

"Excuse me?"

"Know who I was." He watched her eyes widen and her mouth open with surprise.

"You haven't changed a bit. I'd have recognized you thirty years from now. I had a lot of time to think about it. And I had all afternoon to figure out how I was going to approach you, because I wasn't sure you weren't playing with me. I just didn't think this 'high level' group," she said using her fingers as quotes, "wouldn't have figured it out first, and that bothered me. So that should tell you how well they've vetted everything, including your helpers here. A lot can happen in a week. Something's wrong."

Again, she was smartly assessing their situation. And she'd successfully steered the conversation away from the interpersonal cloud that still remained between them. He hoped trusting her intuitions wouldn't wind them into some unforeseen danger. But he wanted to in the worst way.

"So, what do *you* think happened?" he asked.

Mimi hesitated, putting her fingers against the glass on the window overlooking the woods.

"She spent a lot of time texting boys, sending pictures, but they all do that." She turned to face him. "I didn't worry about it because I was reassured her phone had security locks on it, so only 'vetted' –there's that word again—people could contact her." She smiled, looking down at her feet as she leaned against the window sill.

"Go on." He liked watching her talk.

"Somehow, she found a way to get free. I think that's all she wanted, a little slice of a normal life somewhere. I don't think it has anything to do with politics or even her parents. She wanted to take back her life."

"So, you think she initiated this, then?"

She nodded her head. "My hunch is yes. Or at least it's a theory we have to explore."

Mimi was way smarter than he'd given her credit for earlier. Her in-depth assessment of their target was just as detailed as some he'd received in the theater by well-trained, seasoned CIA operatives.

"Unfortunately," he answered softly, "she has no idea what the real world is like or how much danger she's in."

Her honest gaze let him know she understood completely. They were both on the same page, finally.

"It's the same problem with all celebrity kids. I had three whole classes with them and got used to dealing with their parents, who had enough money to buy whole countries, or start a revolution. It was hard telling their parents they needed to check on their kid's homework, even though their company was in the process of being overtaken in a hostile bid, or their country was at war."

He considered all this, forming a grid pattern in his own mind. He began to fill in the boxes that had question marks in them earlier. It was too soon to show her. He hoped she'd make the team, because he knew she'd add a lot.

Of course, there was that personal angle. He trusted her. He knew he'd do everything he could to protect her too. But who was going to protect him from his own heart? He knew the signs, and he was going to try to stuff those thoughts down. And what would he do if DHS said the mission was scrapped or they needed to put someone *else* in charge because of that history?

It was going to be one of those days when the next few hours would mean success or failure. He definitely had a preference. But it wasn't entirely his decision.

AFTER DINNER, GARRETT took a call he'd requested from Branson.

"We have a complication, Si."

"Already? Shit, you don't like the house? The Suburban doesn't have enough gadgets?"

"I need you to know that Mrs. Wagner is really Connor Lambert's daughter."

"Christ in a handbag."

"How did that slip by, Silas?"

"Now you know what we've been working under. Some of our intelligence gathering is grossly misnamed."

"So how accurate is your intel if you don't even have the right deets on the potential team?"

Silas let out a gasp he'd tried to hide. "Well, she's still the one who has most the information on Sorrel. That part you're not disputing, are you?"

"No. That part's fine. More than fine. She's a good source and she's more stable than I thought originally. Now that I know where she comes from, it isn't a problem for me, but I wanted you to be aware."

"Go with your gut. I'm not taking this up the command."

"You sure about that? This could be a trap."

"Hell, if it's a trap, we're all fucked, Garrett."

He hung up the phone and lay back on his bed, knowing that if he didn't keep himself in check the complication could become a major snake pit.

God, he hated snakes.

CHAPTER 6

MIMI HAD A fitful night. She knew it would get resolved in time, but the added pressure of the minutes ticking away made her crazy. In addition, adrenaline created by her excitement at seeing Garrett again, and perhaps being able to be a part of his team, didn't give her room to sleep. She wanted to impress him, and that made her uneasy. She didn't want to try too hard, but found the more time she spent around him, the more comfortable and surer she was about what she was doing. She hoped he felt the same.

She'd moved to D.C. to get away from all the SEAL stuff. But here she was, again, immersed in it up to her eyebrows. Except when she was a child, when her dad went off to parts unknown, she'd know practically nothing about the mission or even where he was going. She did remember the way he'd take her in his arms, be gentle until her shaking body calmed, and promise everything was going to be okay. He'd whisper instructions about listening to her mom.

"You're tougher than she is, Maggie," he'd say as he touched the top of her head. His warm purring voice had been so consoling she could do nothing else but agree. But after he had driven off down the street, and she watched him every time she had a chance to, she was left with an unspeakable void. But it was nothing compared to the emptiness she felt when he had been permanently taken from them.

Being honest with herself, she acknowledged that Garrett had that same tender voice, that reassuring confidence.

Careful.

Warning signs and dark clouds were beginning to form at the corners of her mind, but she needed to indulge herself just a little longer. She'd gone years without having her dad. She'd risk the danger that perhaps her attraction to Garrett had something to do with that. It was confusing. But she pushed all those thoughts away, telling herself she needed to be mindful of the mission to find Georgette. It was what her dad would have recommended.

"Focus on the goal, Maggie. Just keep your head focused on what's most important, and everything else will slip into place. Trust yourself but work to concentrate so you aren't blindsided. You can do it. You're just like me."

The sunshine raining in through the large dining room window was the best feature of the house, she thought. Mist was still swirled through the tall trees. The ground was becoming carpeted with the orange and gold tones of fall. The more she stared into the woods, the more she felt that something was out there, ready to come towards her. Something in her future was about to be revealed between these trees.

"Coffee?" Garrett's voice shook her to reality.

"Love some."

He handed her a mug, already filled with cream and no sugar. "Just guessing on the condiments."

"Yup," she said as she supped. "Just like my dad. That means you must have gotten half and half."

"Hell no. Heavy cream. I think he must have kept that a secret from you."

The coffee was soothing. She sat where they'd had their conversation last night. "What's happening today? Any news?"

"We're getting a White House staff briefing this morning. The guy should be here any minute now. I've also got some new potential candidates for the team." He was smiling down on her.

After he sat and set his coffee down, he leaned back on the leather couch and crossed his legs.

"I'm letting you ask questions, if you want to, Mimi."

She nearly spit out her coffee. "Really?" She wrinkled her nose and pushed her glasses back onto the bridge of her nose. "Wow. I didn't know you thought much of what I said last night."

"I think you can pick up some things I'll miss. And you don't have to speak up, if you don't want to. Just offering you the chance, if you think it's important."

"Okay, I will. These are people you know? You've worked with them before?"

"The potential members? Yes, all but one. And the White House staffer I've never met before, either."

"Our boys will be back?"

"Oh yes, got them running errands this morning. I'm warming to them." He smiled to his mug.

She knew he was about to ask her a question he wasn't sure about. She waited, watching him rub the knuckles of his left hand.

"Can I ask you a question about your husband?"

"Sure."

"What Team?"

"Three or five. He was working up to be on either of them, depending on the rotation, and who they needed."

"Kyle Lansdowne is one of the LPOs of Team 3, good friend of mine."

"I met him and his wife. Also met several from Team 5. All good guys."

"Surprised they let you get out of San Diego without bringing a SEAL with you to D.C.?"

It was the truth and Jason had warned her about that. When one member doesn't make it home, someone else steps in to fill the spot. "I wasn't up to dating. I needed my space and a fresh start. Everything in Coronado reminded me of too many happier times. It was a quick decision to get married, and it was over before I could get into a routine."

"And yet you married him."

"I was going through some things with my mom at the time and was thinking about leaving. Then I met him. We dated a few times and I liked him. He asked me, and I said yes without thinking."

She'd wrestled with the guilt of knowing deep inside perhaps she didn't love him as she wanted to. Surely Garrett knew all about quick decisions and weddings before deployment.

"Just so you don't think I'm a terrible person, I know I would have grown to love him. I think I was just lonely, and wanted some stability. We should have waited until he got back, but he insisted, and I wanted to get settled too, so I thought it would work. And it probably would have."

The weight of Garrett's eyes on her was heavy. Well, at least, she was being honest.

"I'm sorry," he whispered softly.

She could finally bring herself to look back at him. "We were very happy in that brief time. It was just a freak accident right after we got married. These things always happen to other people. We never expect them to in our lives, do we?"

Garrett nodded, and waited for her to continue.

"After, I knew I had to get out of San Diego, or I'd go insane. So, I applied around, and got this job."

She was grateful for the knock at the door.

Garrett's body traversed the living room in three long strides, welcoming a small crowd of several men standing on the porch outside.

"Fuzzy! Look at you!" he said as he hugged a bald man about his own age, built like a wrestler, with tatted forearms. Mimi thought he resembled a modern-day Popeye, without the pipe.

The man brushed the top of his head with his palm. "Well, I finally gave up. I don't believe all that man-hood shit."

His quick glance in Mimi's direction put a palm to his mouth.

"Excuse me, ma'am."

"Get in here," Garrett said as he yanked his arm inside, and then greeted the others, one by one. All of them were lean but muscled. Two were clean-cut like Fuzzy, but one had long hair pulled into a ponytail. "Joshua, welcome aboard. Look at you, Luke. Glad to have you on the team, Tanner." The last man extended his hand.

"Cornell Bigelow. Pleased to meet you Commander." His handsome dark face lit up with a warm smile.

"Just Garrett. Derek gave you high marks. I'm still working on getting him, but thanks for showing up."

"Thanks. I'm real honored to be here."

"Okay, go upstairs and pick your rooms," Garrett barked the instructions. "All of them are upstairs. Leave the one downstairs vacant. I'm asking you to pair up, but nobody shares with me, or Mimi, here."

The group faced her. She could see the questions rising through crusty grins. She walked toward them extending her hand.

"I'm Mimi Wagner. I was Georgette's teacher at the Academy. I understand I've been asked to be part of this at the request of Georgette's mother—"

"—And father, don't forget POTUS," corrected Garrett.

Someone whistled. Fuzzy asked her, "You tight with the First Lady?"

"Not at all. I've only met her twice at school functions and only once have we been introduced."

"I'll bet those would be interesting parent-teacher conferences," Fuzzy answered to the group, who chuckled.

Of course, Mimi wasn't going to reveal anything

about the lack of conferences, or the fact that all the updates went to staffers. But that's the way it was, and as a First Family, they knew there were sacrifices, even if Georgette didn't.

That was the problem.

"Hey, Fuzzy, you're a bit out of line," Garrett barked. "No politics here. No opinions, either. Especially yours!"

"She might be the First Lady, but she's a mother, just like all our mothers were," said the one identified as Joshua. "And I know she worries about her daughter no more, no less."

"Exactly," added Garrett. "What their lifestyle is has no bearing on what we're doing here, nor should it. Everyone clear on that?"

Fuzzy shrugged his agreement, and the others nodded.

A black Suburban pulled up outside as the group began to disperse.

Garrett went out to the stoop to introduce himself to their new visitor.

A skinny mid-thirties nerd extricated himself from the vehicle, hauling a briefcase. Behind him, his military driver brought two other pieces of equipment in thick grey hard case boxes. He stopped to shake Garrett's hand at the doorway.

"Mike Bintner, White House Security, sir. I'm here

to be your White House liaison."

"No need for any formalities. I'm Garrett Tierney, and glad to have you here."

Once inside, he introduced her. Mimi thought the briefcase-toting special agent didn't fit in with the rest of the group.

The boxes were set by the doorway and the driver left.

"So where do you want to get set up?" Garrett asked.

"I better explain what's going on first. Those," he pointed to the cases, "Are from Branson. I have nothing to do with that, so they stay there. I—I think you've been issued some weaponry."

"Okay, cool."

"But I do have some videos and images I need to share with you. You all should take a look at these, I think."

Garrett whistled for the others to join them downstairs.

"I normally have a big screen to use, so you'll have to crowd in to see, but I got some footage you'll find interesting."

He opened his laptop and clicked through to a stilled video, making it full screen.

"We looked over everything Sorrell did for the past two weeks, and then we expanded it to include the president and the First Lady. Sorrell had her normal routine, going to school, without any field trips, or side trips. As far as we know, she didn't even take her team shopping, which is one of the things she likes to do. She appeared to be studying, in her room most the time. We don't surveil her inside the family quarters, of course. But no one had access to her other than staff, and her parents, at least not that we know of."

"Okay, so where does this leave us?" Garrett asked.

"Let me show you in a minute. Aside from previously-approved tour groups always cycling through the White House, and some foreign dignitaries, which were well-supervised, nothing appeared to involve the First Daughter. Until we came to this."

He clicked the video and Mimi could see a large ballroom filled with tables and people filing in to occupy seats at these tables.

"This was the White House Prayer Breakfast, which was held two weeks ago."

Mimi remembered that day since several of her students were not in class, including Georgette.

"And that table right there," he pointed to one in the upper right corner, "has a number of college-aged kids. If you look carefully, you can see Georgette there."

Unlike the elusive starry-eyed dreamer Mimi usually had in class, Georgette was throwing her head back, laughing, and leading in the conversations. The whole table was animated and appeared to be having a good deal of fun.

"Is it customary for Sorrell to attend such events?" Asked Garrett.

"Sometimes. It just depends. She wasn't on the original roster and seating chart. I remember having to juggle a bit. Rather than move someone to an adult table—sorry, that's just how we see it—we kept all the youths together."

Mimi also noticed that the table was clear across the room from the president and First Lady's table. She tried to identify the kids and couldn't recognize any of them as being Georgette's friends from school.

"What do you see, Mimi?" Garrett asked.

"Well, I was just thinking that none of her school friends are there. Usually, if she has to go to one of these functions, she's got someone or maybe two others with her. There two others in my class that were excused for a White House event that day, but I don't see them here. In fact, I've not seen any of these kids here," she touched the screen at several of the attendees, "anywhere around our campus, either. They're all strangers to me."

"So, let's find out who they are, Mike," Garrett asked.

"Already anticipated that one, Commander." He

produced a printout. "All the attendees and their affiliations. And I also brought this. It has just the breakfast footage on it. But it's the entire event, even the president's speech. I've not been given authority to give you anything else." He held up a thumb drive and handed it to Garrett.

"Cool beans." Garrett placed the drive in his pocket.

Joshua Lopez, who had been introduced as FBI, asked to see the list. His forefinger scanned the names and affiliations. "You've got POG here. A number of others I don't recognize, but I'm surprised to see the POG folks here. And none of the kids have affiliations."

Mike bit his lower lip. "My concern exactly. I think we have it somewhere, because everyone there would be vetted. I'm guessing someone else on the staff was responsible for that. I'll get that for you when we locate it."

"What's POG?" asked Fuzzy.

"They're a fringe evangelical group, small but vocal, I hear," answered Mike. "But big supporters of the president. That's how they got in."

"You remember that encampment in Texas who were causing trouble some years back?" Joshua said to the others. "Turned out to be a tax case, but initially they were into multiple wives and arranged marriages.

They were forced out of their compound."

"That's right," remarked Luke. "During the Harris administration. His attorney general was from Texas. But I thought the group disbanded. The Bureau was all over them."

"That's what I thought too," said Joshua.

"Okay, so we focus on them for starters. Anyone else, Josh? Anything that looks funny?" asked Garrett.

"I'll get to work right away on those, sir. But you definitely want to get that list from Georgette's table." He addressed Mike next. "Was she seen with any of these kids afterwards on any of the footage?"

"Nope. No one that I can tell has visited her afterwards either. We monitor and track the calls, and we've already been over all those. She's pretty restricted."

"And still no ransom demands, strange calls or packages to POTUS or FLOTUS?"

Mimi had to work on herself to stop from giggling.

"Not so far. It's really creepy. Very unusual. We've expanded the group a bit, so we have more eyes on everything, but they don't know about the Bone Frog Command, trust me on that. I've made it clear that's not to go outside my handful of agents and only a few trusted White House staff I know and have worked with," answered Mike.

"Good work," said Garrett. "Wish there were more

results, but I think we're on to something here. Just a hunch."

The team asked questions about protocol, scheduling, and quiet monitoring of the staff.

He gave them his team's contact information. "Anything else you need, let me know."

"I have a request," asked Mimi. "Can I have access to Georgette's room for a few minutes? I just want to look around, see if I can pick up on anything?"

"Sure, but let me get okay from the family first. And we'll have to make up a ruse to get you in there or there will be gossip from the staff. A small handful know she's missing, but we're trying to keep that number small to keep it out of the press."

"I think that's a great suggestion, and, Mike, the sooner the better," said Garrett.

After Mike left, the new members of the team introduced themselves to each other.

"Well I'm Luke Sorvay," he said with his Louisiana drawl. "Been with the Bureau for over twenty, now doing State Department Special Agent temporary assignments. But I started out as a froglet under Tierney's command. I was one and done, mostly because we started having kids and my wife didn't take too kindly to me being away when they were born."

"Luke here is a hell of a medic. We missed him when he left," added Garrett.

"Thank you, sir."

"Joshua, your turn," said Garrett.

"Joshua Lopez. I've done just about everything. After the Marines, I worked undercover for the Gang Task Force, with the Bureau. I've embedded with some scary dudes in Central America involved in human trafficking and drugs."

He locked eyes with Mimi, which gave her a fright.

"My wife doesn't like it that I can still pose as a drug dealer in his twenties and I turned forty this year."

Everyone laughed.

"I'm Tanner Janssen, and after five tours, decided Homeland Security would pay better than the Army did, so I switched over about ten years ago. I'm working on cyber security, surveillance of certain subjects and groups. Was hoping to retire this year, dammit," he said as he punched Garrett in the arm.

"What do you mean, this is retirement, right?" Garrett smiled. "And now, we got another jarhead, Fuzzy Kinski."

"That's me. I'm a New Jersey cop now, and hell, I had already signed my retirement papers, but I couldn't turn down old Garrett here. In the Marines, we did a lot of hostage rescue, embassy support in some strange places we shouldn't even have an embassy. Met Garrett on one of my tours and we've been friends ever since. I'm a widower now, which makes me a mean motherfucker!"

Again, the group laughed.

"Excuse me again, ma'am," he added.

"Mimi, you go next," asked Garrett.

"Well—"

She turned to Garrett and wondered how much of their past she should reveal. He gave her no encouragement or indication. She was going to have to wing it.

"I grew up in San Diego. My father served on SEAL Team 3 until he was killed in Afghanistan when I was fourteen. I met Garrett as I was growing up." She squinted at him. "I think I was around 6 when we first met. He was my dad's best friend."

She gulped in air and tried to continue without her voice wavering, but her emotions were building.

"I looked for a change of scenery after I lost my husband and took this job last year at the Academy. I've gotten to know Georgette Collier as well as I guess anyone, and I think we formed a special bond, if that doesn't sound too cocky. I'm here without any formal training like you guys, but I can help because of what I know. I can shoot, but not very well."

"They didn't tell me that," interrupted Garrett.

Everyone laughed.

Mimi raised her eyebrows and smirked, embarrassed at the focused attention she was getting. "I don't do karate or any kind of sports, don't bench press or lift weights. Don't ask me to run a 5k or run to the store. I'm not your girl."

The group chuckled again.

"I love reading, novels, poetry and especially romance novels. Some day when I get tired of teaching, maybe I'll write a book."

They clapped, which mortified her.

"Cornell?"

"I had the distinction of working on several joint ops with several SEAL Teams, on a TDA when they were short a man. I did ten on the teams and then went to the CIA, then private contractor work, mostly security. And I hear you, Tanner, about the pay. We've also done hostage rescue, mostly embassy staffers and American citizens caught in the crosshairs. On the teams, my specialty was sharpshooting."

"We're trying to get his buddy Derek Farley on board, but he's got some obligations he trying to work out. You know the guy, the SEAL Celebrity Chef?"

Mimi had never heard of him.

An hour later, everyone was working in their rooms or on their laptops at the dining table, when they got the call from Mike that she could inspect Georgette's room in the White House. He asked her to bring some wallpaper books so she could pose as a decorator.

And Garrett was to accompany her.

While their team began the assignments, Garrett and Mimi headed out for one of the area's home decorating stores on their way to the White House.

"Looks like you'll get to add one more thing to your resume, Garrett," Mimi said.

He kept his eyes on the road but frowned. "What's that?"

"Have you ever measured for drapes?" she asked him.

"I don't have drapes in my house," he answered, still not looking at her.

"And that doesn't surprise me a bit. Just don't trip and fall when we get there. You gotta look like a pro, and pros don't damage furniture."

"I'm more civilized than that," he said, turning his face to her.

They shared a smile. Mimi felt an electric chill quiver down her spine.

CHAPTER 7

G ARRETT SAT ON the two-step ladder they'd bought from the paint store. The White House staff had left so they were left alone in Georgette's room with Mike Bintner. Garrett set the measuring tape on the bedside table. Mimi lay down her new clipboard and adjusted her glasses, surveying the room.

Mike handed both of them sterile gloves and placed a pair on himself as well. "You have to use these at all times in here."

It made him feel like he was at a crime scene.

It struck Garrett that this looked more like a room in a hotel than the bedroom of a celebrity teenager. It was devoid of posters, except for one large bulletin board, where Georgette had posted pictures with friends, events she was planning on attending and photos she'd cut out from magazines and other sources.

"My sister had junk all over the walls," he remarked.

Mimi headed for Georgette's desk, and pointed, asking permission to inspect it.

Mike nodded, then addressed him. "The wallpaper here is of historical value. I guess in the past some White House kids have tried to paint over or strip the paper away. She had her choice of rooms. This one had the French Blue paper that is over a hundred years old, so they allowed her the bulletin board."

Mimi sat down on the teen's chair and began to review items on her desktop.

"You have taken her computer?" she asked.

"Yes, we've got it, inspected it. We're monitoring it as well in her absence."

"And her phone?"

"We have that as well. If she'd taken it with her, we could have tracked her down. But she left it behind. It has a tracking device, as I'm sure you'd imagine."

Garrett felt a little sheepish. He'd inspected hovels overseas, sifting through personal effects and papers, even private compartments of some Heads of State, without thinking twice. But never had he examined a young American girl's things, let alone the president's daughter. And of course, he'd never posed as a decorator, carrying fabric samples and a wallpaper book, with a tape measure clipped to his belt. The light blue flowered motif was such a delicate backdrop to the dangerous possibilities of what danger Georgette could be facing.

Garrett started looking over the posters she'd displayed, handling things carefully through the gloves. There were several postcards sent by friends from exotic places. He examined the backsides and didn't find anything that interested him. "You've looked these over, I suppose?" He asked Mike.

"You got it. Besides, all those cards are brought in through the White House Security process. Every piece of mail she would have received is scanned, dusted and opened before it gets here."

He flipped over a card from a winery in Sonoma County, where his house was located and noted one of her friends wrote about a family vacation there. She had her class schedule posted, and a calendar, Garrett noting some of the entries were in different styles of writing.

He wondered how he would have felt as a teen, growing up so watched and monitored. There were definitely some things he did that he never wanted his mother to know about. Would Georgette feel the same?

He looked up to find Mimi engrossed in a book.

"WHAT'D YOU FIND?" he asked.

"She's got a diary here."

"Where did you find that?" asked Mike.

"It looks like a Bible. But I scanned the pages. At the end, there are about forty or so pages of blanks for notes. She's been keeping a diary for—let's see, this is not quite a month now."

Mike stood behind her, reading over her shoulder.

"I honestly didn't see this. We thought we had all her diaries. Good job, Mimi."

"Anything interesting?" Garrett asked.

"Well, she starts out saying this was a gift." Mimi looked up at both of them. "Could she have been given this at the prayer breakfast?"

"We didn't see anything on the recordings." Mike leaned forward and put his forefinger on the spine. "There's a page missing, see it?"

Garrett also looked over Mimi's shoulder and saw the remnants of a blank piece of notebook removed. Mike picked it up and splayed his fingers over the writing Georgette had done, then held it up, examining it closer.

"We're going to have to send this in. Be careful with the pages, but let's read it over carefully, then I'll bag it."

Mimi read aloud. Garrett stood back, then sat back down on the ladder, unsure whether he should sit on any of the furniture.

'*What a surprise to get this special gift. I promise to write in it every day! I'm reading the passages here too.*

Loren will be so proud of me! I told him I'm a bad girl in training, but he said if I studied this book, I'd change. Will this make me a good girl now? Some days I wonder if it's too late. But I'm going to try. There is so much I want to do and so much I can't. So, these are just some private thoughts for me, and me alone. I want to do something with my life that means something, and this is where I'll start. Shhh!!! Don't tell anyone!'

Mimi looked up at him. "Who's Loren?"

"Must be one of the kids at her table. I don't recall ever seeing a name like that. Could be a boy or a girl."

"I'm guessing boy," answered Mimi.

"What day was that?" Mike asked.

"October 2," Mimi read.

"That's the day after the breakfast," said Mike.

"And look at this, Mike, there are passages high-lighted."

"We saw those, just missed the notebook," he answered. "Now I'm going to study them closer."

Mimi flipped to the back of the book. She read a few more passages. Four days into the entries there was a break for two days, then she resumed. The passages became worrisome as Mimi read out,

'He maketh me to lie down in green pastures. He fulfills my soul. And then she's paraphrasing again, *I will go through the valley of the shadow of death and I will fear no evil.'*

Garret's concern was deepening. "Holy cow. She's met someone. Someone she's following. We gotta find this Loren character."

"I think you're right," answered Mimi. "It's like someone has used the Bible passages to conform them to a plan, a messiah-like plan. And they've misquoted the good book as well."

"But for what end?" Garrett posed.

"It's not good. None of this is good," whispered Mike. "It's not the Bible verses themselves, but her or someone else's interpretation of them. Someone's affixed a meaning where there wasn't one intended. This is manipulation."

The door to the bedroom opened. Garrett grabbed his tape measure out of reflex. Mimi and Mike were frozen in position.

"Mr. President," remarked Mike.

"Stay as you are. Liz is on her way as well. We just wanted to get a quick update, if you don't mind." Harrison Collier's face looked ashen, his cheeks sunken and his eyes puffy. Garrett noticed the toll it had taken on the normally tanned and vibrant-looking man.

The president shook Garrett's hand. "Mr. President," he said. "I'm so sorry about all this."

"Call me Harrison. And yes, this is one of the things I never imagined would happen to us here. But, I have heard a lot about your heroics. I'm glad Liz was able to get you on this special team."

Garrett knew Branson had been the real person to have chosen him but wasn't going to correct the president.

"Thank you, sir. I'm going to do everything I was trained to get this mission accomplished as quickly as I can, sir. It's an honor."

"Bone Frog. That Branson's choice?" the president asked. Garrett noticed his undereyes were dark and he suspected it was from lack of sleep.

"That's a term for old SEALs," Garrett was nervous and didn't want to tell him it defined departed ones as well. "I guess I'm old enough to wear that. Got a little gray, and such," he said as he felt his face flush.

"Well I'm just a bit older than you are, so I must make me an old guy, ancient. Better watch it!" the president said, laughing. But the laugh was strained, and Garrett could see laughter was a nervous cure for how sick he must feel inside. He couldn't imagine the man's pain.

Just then, the First Lady slipped inside and closed the door behind her. Mimi stood, handing the bible to Mike.

Liz Collier was even more beautiful than her photographs. Garrett had seen her before, but from afar. She was well-toned, with light blonde hair cascading in curls over her shoulders. Garrett was tongue-tied.

She came right over to him. "I'm so glad you're going to help us, Garrett." Her eyes sparkled, but he could see noticeable puffiness and new tears forming. She was also straining to keep up a happy countenance. Her brittle smile was followed by a slight wink as she continued. "Felicia has told me so much about you. I feel like we've met."

Garrett was frozen in place, until he realized she'd extended her hand and he was expected to shake it.

"Ma'am. I was just telling The president here I'll do everything within my power to get her back safe, and quickly, if it's possible."

She gave his hand an extra squeeze before she released him. Then she brushed something from her right eye and stood by her husband, taking his hand.

Garrett finally found his voice. "I believe you know your daughter's teacher, Mimi Wagner?"

Mimi approached tentatively, and then took Mrs. Collier's hand. "Good to see you again, but I'm so sorry for the circumstances. This must be hell for you both." Mimi added, "We're going to work night and day to find her. You have the very best man here, for the job."

"Thank you," both the president and his wife whispered in return.

Garrett was surprised at Mimi's flattery.

"Well, what have you found so far?" the president asked.

"Sir, we're kind of focusing on the Prayer Breakfast. Could there be any chance she met someone there that we aren't aware of?" Mike asked the couple.

"Not that I noticed. It was run through the staff, with Secret Service input, invitation only," Collier said. "I'm sure they were all checked out."

"How about the kids table?" Garrett asked.

"Well most of these kids are sons and daughters of the pastors or their staff who attended. I think it's safe to say this would be one of the safest groups ever to come here. We've never had any issues or problems going back through several administrations," he continued. "Or so I've been told."

"Is there any reason you're focusing on this particular event?" Mrs. Collier asked him.

"Mimi found a diary at the back of a bible that appears to have been a gift she may have gotten at the breakfast from a Loren. Does that ring any bells? We're wondering if one of the kids gave it to her," answered Mike.

"A diary?" Liz Collier questioned. "Can I see it?"

Mike held it up. "We're wearing protective gloves. I'm going to have it analyzed for prints. I'd be happy to have copies of her pages delivered to you, but right now, I want to get it to the Bureau."

"But have you read it? What does she say about this Loren person?" Mrs. Collier was getting agitated.

"Mrs. Collier," Mimi started. "She talks about that someone gave it to her, just talks about doing something important with her life. These are all things I've seen before with my students, even in some of her writing in my class."

Garrett felt the need to jump in, "So far, nothing in the writing that is of much interest. But the prints are more important. If we can find out who gave it to her, it might shed some light on things."

"Did she indicate she was unhappy?" the president asked. "I just don't understand how this could happen. Any indication she may have planned this? Or that she was depressed?"

"We don't know, sir," Garrett added. "I wish I could be more definitive. But think about the breakfast and before. Anything unusual that transpired there? Anything about the guest list that was unusual?"

They both shook their heads, solemnly.

THE TRIP BACK to the house was long. Mimi fell asleep against the window and then woke up as they turned off the freeway and began threading through the wooded countryside.

He was anxious, even though he'd only been part of the team for the second day. He was hoping when he got back, that the team had dug up something they could go on, some lead they could follow.

Today was productive, and it gave him some direction. But he was angered at the pace.

Mimi turned to him. "You think they're hiding something?"

"I have no clue." He shrugged and thought about her question. "Why, you pick up on anything?"

"Not sure, but didn't you think it was odd the president asked about whether she was depressed? Do you suppose she's had some issues we don't know about?"

"Well, you know her. What do you think?"

"I was struck by two things today. First, I was surprised they didn't find that journal in the Bible. And second, I get the feeling someone isn't telling the truth. It would sure make it a whole lot easier to find her if we knew who and why. That's my thought." She looked back at him with her honest eyes.

He decided not to reveal to her that he agreed. That was the point. Someone was trying to impede their forward motion. It felt like some of those missions where they walked into an ambush. Again, the intel was lacking, just like Branson had said.

But he knew, if given the time and the tools, once they found out what the real score was, the team would be making a relentless bid to get it solved and get her home safe.

If that was possible.

CHAPTER 8

THE BLARE OF heavy metal rock music hit her from behind the large oak door even before Mimi and Garrett stepped back into the house. But once they entered the foyer, the scene was straight from her college days.

The dining room table had become a kind of geek lab, with some of the team wearing earphones and rocking out to their own private beats while others danced as they typed and manipulated their gadgets. A big screen had been mounted crooked on the wall.

Fuzzy had on a muscle shirt and drawstring shorts and was covered in sweat, looking like he'd just come from a run. His tats covering his arms and lower legs moved like wild animals, his calves as large as tree trunks. He was also smoking a cigar, which had managed to give the whole room's air a light blue watercolor wash. "Hey boss!" he yelled, waving to Garrett.

Tanner had set up a folding table to the side. On it were several devices Mimi didn't recognize. Heat signals and scratchy voice communications she'd only seen in movies caught her attention. More fascinating was the beanie cap with a propeller on it Tanner displayed on his head, and since he wore headsets, they partially hung up one of the propellers. He was so engrossed in his work that he had no idea they had entered the room.

Cornell Bigelow, the former SEAL, former CIA private contractor, sported a cap with dreadlocks. His expensive all-black workout suit was completely devoid of symbols or patches, his eyes hidden behind dark glasses. He fist-power saluted both of them.

Joshua's long hair was in a ponytail while he Latin danced to the heavy guitar and drum music. Shades, a Red Friday tee shirt, camo pants, and flip flops completed his ensemble.

Luke Sorvay was the only one in a golf shirt, tan slacks, and tennis shoes. He looked like he'd just come from the bar at a country club, though his club cap was backwards.

Mimi saw Garrett's shocked expression.

"Holy crap," he said, under his breath. "This better mean we have some good news."

"Oh yes, we have some very good news, Cap'n," said Fuzzy. "Tell them, Tanner."

"We got a ping on her cell. Someone tried to call her. The guys just called me. Joshua has some further info on this location too. The ping came from a location in Oregon, unless it's a bleeder." Tanner's face bore a wide grin like he was a five-year-old losing his first tooth.

"Bleeder?" asked Garrett.

"Bread crumbs. A trail, usually false. But they didn't stay long, leaving a message, so doesn't look like a deliberate plant. Someone could be trying to reach her. Part of the crew who took her, or someone she was supposed to meet up with?" Tanner's happy expression was a welcomed sight.

Fuzzy interrupted. "Except if they took her, they'd know they left her cell behind. And the reason they didn't take it is because her phone doesn't have any contact information on them. So I'm not thinking it would not be someone she was supposed to contact within the group." Fuzzy took a drag on his gnarled cigar and blew the smoke to the ceiling.

Mimi was going to have to keep her distance since cigar smoke gave her a ginormous headache.

"Good point," said Garrett.

Tanner agreed and said so.

"That makes total sense," added Joshua.

The two of them approached the table. Garrett inspected what they'd set up, including studying the post-it charts plastered to the walls, brainstormed ideas, and a blow-up of Garrett's grid with the question marks and blanks they had to fill in.

The variety of equipment fascinated Mimi, as well as the number of highly specialized power cords snaking all over the table and the floor. She also noticed the mounting of the large screen had been done by clumsily directly drilling into the wall and wondered whether there would be a complaint about that.

"So I'm thinking it was Georgette, and I'll tell you more in a minute. She could be trying to make contact," said Joshua.

Garrett angled his head and squinted down on her. She nodded without him asking her.

"I think you're right," she whispered.

"Does she have your cell number?" he asked.

"She does."

Garrett's face reflected his love for this sort of mission, how the action of a joint task force invigorated him, just like she remembered her father had described. As she scanned the men in front, they all had that same level of excitement, showing it in slightly different ways, but all reflecting a positive energy connection between themselves and the desire and confidence to bring success. She could see why they loved it. Why her father could never stop.

"And look at this. I dug up information on the POG group and some sketchy stuff on the kid's table." His face showed a frown. He was choosing his words carefully. "Garrett, any reason why this info has to take so long to get to us and why it comes piecemeal?"

Garret and Mimi shared a glance.

"We've already talked about this. Noted."

Fuzzy spoke up. "In defense of the White House, I'll say that sometimes things slip through. You wouldn't believe some of the lapses we had in Embassy security. They often err on the side of a big donor or someone who has promised a favor to the administration. We had enemy combatants in some of our meetings overseas, but our ambassador wanted to include them because they were trying to work with them. It's just a risk assessment."

"But surely not in the White House—" Joshua began.

"*Especially* in the White House," Luke Sorvay barked.

Joshua swore in Spanish.

"Cash is king," Luke continued. "There might not have been enough time. These events don't get planned, except for the date, longer than two to three weeks. A lot of juggling goes on. Just happens," he added as he shrugged.

"If someone wants to get close to the president, being at a harmless prayer breakfast would be a good way to get in. And if they are a big donor, all the easier," Fuzzy continued.

Mimi felt uneasy with all this. Her impression was that the security, especially security at the White House, was like in a supermax prison. Now she realized that the only persons who felt restricted were those who lived there. For everyone else, ways existed to obtain entry. The First Family carried the burden of that knowledge with them all day long.

She knew it would weigh on Georgette, who was just trying to be a normal teenager.

"In protective detail, we can't stop every event. We just have to be faster in the response and try to eliminate all the variables. That's the mission. But it's never one hundred percent," said Luke.

"Shit, it's like a sieve in there," whispered Cornell Bigelow. "They could be sitting ducks."

"My friends at Treasury say it's the same way at the Federal Reserve Banks," added Luke. "They can't stop the theft, but they can make it take a long time to get out and hope that one of the checkpoints will discover the theft of cash or securities."

"Or increase the number of insiders needed to pull it off," grumbled Fuzzy.

Garrett was nodding. "So, Josh, there's your answer. Some butt-covering going on. Whomever was assigned to her team may not have done the job like he was supposed to, and they aren't willing to come clean about it."

"Gotcha. Well, here's what I got on POG, and actually I got more out of the internet than anywhere else. After the Texas shut-down, Nelson Bales and his group,"—Joshua posted the picture of a handsome middle-aged man, looking more like a movie star than a pastor, on the large screen—"moved to a town outside of Klamath Falls. They've kept a pretty low profile there. Stayed off social media, except for some goodwill doing during the recent Oregon and California fires. Keeping their noses clean, or so it seems."

Joshua flipped several images across the screen of the group handing out food, clothing, furniture, and other things, plus setting up soup kitchens and donating fresh produce.

"They live in a secluded little valley—and you're gonna love this. *Used* to be a terrorist training camp some of your buddies on Team 3 shut down a few years ago. Property went up for auction after everyone either left the country or went to prison."

Pictures continued flashing on the screen. Views of well-tended gardens and greenhouses, well-stocked kitchens, and happy workers with big smiles on their faces repeated one by one until the collage of goodwill gestures became overwhelming.

"You got all this on the internet? That doesn't sound like they have kept a low profile," said Tanner.

"Not from their site. I searched the group and found most of these from articles written about them in local online papers, or joint partners when there were donations being asked for fire victims. They partnered with lots of groups, even Red Cross, police and fire volunteers, in a supportive role, of course," he answered.

"Are you impressed yet, Garrett?" chortled Fuzzy.

"I'm beginning to think you guys do better without me. This is an excellent start. Way more than I had anticipated. Now, let's not get blindsided or reach any hasty conclusion, though. We gotta keep an open mind and not rule out anything," Garrett said with pride.

The group agreed. Mimi felt hope spring in her heart they might be able to pull together a rescue plan, and soon.

The hour-long meeting left Mimi exhausted. As they were wrapping up, she cleared the table of the snack plates, chips bags, and dirty dishes, taking a big bag outside to the trash bin in the garage. On the way back, she bumped into Garrett.

"You don't have to do this cleanup, Mimi. Let the guys do some of it."

She smiled back at his face, showing some of the softness she'd seen earlier today.

"I can't stand it. Sorry, Garrett. Just trained to do it. My experience with most men is that if you leave it up to them, it won't get done. Sorry."

He hit his chest like she'd just shot him with an arrow.

She shrugged and slipped past him. Brushing against his side in the narrow space to get to the doorway sent a sizzle to places she'd forgotten about.

As she let the door close behind, she heard him whisper, "Thanks."

AT THREE-THIRTY MIMI received a text message. Her body was tired, and she rolled over when the phone light came on, unable to bring herself to get up. But when it happened a second time, she sat up, suddenly alert, and realized she'd missed the first opportunity. She read the message.

Help me!

She stared down at the screen with the unknown phone number then texted back, *Can you talk? Is this Georgette?*

No and yes. I can text but not long.

Mimi ripped herself out of bed, grabbed the phone and dashed into Garrett's bedroom without knocking. Startled, he came to his feet immediately as she showed him the phone.

In his big hands, the screen lit up again.

Tried calling. Help me escape.

Garrett whispered, "Ask her where she is. How can we contact her other than text?"

Mimi did so. They got the answer.

Somewhere in Oregon. The People Farm. I'm watched. Sorr—

The communication stopped. Several times, Mimi tried to get a response.

"Should I call her?"

"She said not to. Don't want to tip them she's trying to reach out to you."

Mimi then noticed he was wearing his drawstring pajama bottoms in red, white, and blue flags.

But. He. Was. Shirtless.

His hair was disheveled, going in several directions, his beard uncombed, and his neck and cheeks unshaven with salt and pepper stubble showing. His massive shoulders and upper arms formed a mountainous protective barrier between her body and the bed from which he'd just come.

His eyes began to roam down her long-sleeved nightie that she'd unbuttoned quite low and was dangerously gaping. Her legs and thighs were protected from his gaze by the white cotton fabric, but it wasn't flannel. It was fairly see-through. And her hair was thrashing around her face and neck like a wild horse's mane. She could see the view wasn't unpleasant to him.

Then, just as fast as the spark came, it died. His

eyes cooled. He looked to the side and clenched the fist not holding her cell, extending the phone back to her.

"We're gonna have to wait until she messages again. She knows you're willing to talk. Now that she has someone to communicate with, she's going to call back, unless this is a hoax," he whispered. Toward the end of his sentence his eyes softened again as he quickly snuck a peek at her lips.

"Even if it is a hoax, she—or whomever—will call back."

"Exactly what I was thinking," he murmured back carefully.

But Mimi knew exactly what he was thinking, and she was right there with him.

She pushed the phone back to him. "I think it would be better if you kept it. I nearly didn't wake up the first time she texted me. I don't trust myself."

Their fingers touched around the phone. "I'd offer to keep you company, or perhaps you could stay here, and I'd make sure you woke up, but then, I don't trust myself, either."

His eyes drew her in. Something lonely and long-overdue brewed there. Her heart began to race, sending lightning throughout her chest, her midriff, her thighs, and every place in between. Her desire for him had begun to burn in ways she could not ignore any longer.

He was looking at her mouth. Their faces got closer

and closer until his lips brushed across hers and then stopped, pulling slowly away.

She knew she made the choice that would keep her up all night. She didn't follow him but allowed them to part. Still, she had a pretty good notion that her tight nipples had seared a molten hole through her nightgown into his bare chest. Two of his fingers brushed down the side of her thigh as they parted.

It wasn't a wave. It was a greeting and a registration that when she was ready, he would be there.

She quivered, licking her lips.

Suddenly, his arms surrounded her, pulling her to his chest, devouring her lips, searching with his tongue for the treasure they both wanted.

And then it was over.

He abruptly turned, his bare back as beautiful as his front, his scars and tats shining in the moonlight. His strong shoulders reflected the burdens he'd silently carried for so many years. Alone.

He was denying himself again.

And she knew it was the smart thing to do to let him do it a little longer.

"Thank you, Garrett. I'll see you in the morning," she whispered.

She resisted the urge to touch him and just slipped away, out of the room, closing his bedroom door behind her.

The moon kept her up until dawn. The taste of his mouth on hers left her heart racing and the bones of her body ache. She tried to dream but gave up falling asleep. Instead, she replayed visions of make-believe, of what it would feel like to have Garrett's powerful body pleasure her. She knew that she could deliver the same intensity right back.

And rock his world.

CHAPTER 9

G ARRETT SMELLED BACON and eggs cooking downstairs. As he walked past Mimi's room, he noticed
her door was open, bed made, and room straightened,
like a trooper. He heard voices and realized the boy
scouts were here to drop things off he'd requested.
Mimi was making them help her in the kitchen. The
domesticity of it all gave him a warm glow.

All the other bedroom doors were closed, which
meant some of his team had a little too much to drink
the night before. Fuzzy was always the drink master in
any group he'd worked with where excessive alcohol
was involved.

He banged on the cop's door. When he repeated
the blows, he finally got a muffled answer.

"Give me ten more," Fuzzy barked, obviously from
under a pillow.

Garrett found the door locked. "Fuzzy, you open
this door, or I'll bust through."

He heard grumbling. The floor vibrated as if a small herd of baby buffalo stampeded on the other side. Fuzzy appeared, his face red and sweaty, his graying hair springing out to the sides like a clown. The room smelled of farts and body odor. Garrett was disgusted at the condition of one of his most respected long-time friends.

"Sorry, Garrett. That sonofabitch from Louisiana can sure put it down. Looks like a square peg but his tolerance is huge."

"Duly noted." Garrett stared into Fuzzy's red rheumy eyes. "You look like you're twenty years older than you are. A man of contradictions. Smoke cigars but you run. You know the evils of alcohol, but you can drink any of us under the table—"

"Except for Luke."

"Okay, okay. Not arguing. But Fuzzy, I need you here one hundred percent. There's a lot riding on it. I got to have you fit and thinking ahead of me. I can't be dragging your ass to the table."

"You don't have to, Garrett."

"Next time you don't wake up or you ask for another ten minutes of snooze time, you're off the team. I'm pissed and have a right to be. We got a young woman in harm's way and we're the guys who were hired to get her back. Now, get yourself presentable and get your ass downstairs."

"Yessir. It won't happen again."

Garrett banged on the room Joshua and Tanner shared. Tanner appeared, showered and in his underwear. "Got it. We'll be right down. Josh is in the shower."

Before he could get to Cornell and Luke's room, both men stepped into the hallway and ran ahead of him downstairs to their breakfast.

"Understand Fuzzy tried to outdo you, you Cajun freak," Garrett yelled to Luke's backside.

"In his dreams. My mama said she used to give me alcohol as a babe to get me to sleep. I was more familiar with the spirits than my mom's titty juice."

"Do him a favor and don't tempt him again. He's on probation with that stunt."

"Roger that, Garrett. No problems here."

Mimi had arranged a buffet on the kitchen countertop, since the dining table was temporarily overloaded with electronic equipment. He was overwhelmed at the ease with which she moved amongst the men, and how they accepted her in return.

He knew she sensed him standing in the doorway, taking it all in, and she refused to look at him. But she blushed, which was nicer still.

He hadn't forgotten how soft her lips felt, how the smell of her hair and body invited him to press against hers, and how her hot young flesh quivered under his fingers. But he knew these were totally inappropriate thoughts, yet he couldn't stop himself. She wasn't asking anything from him, either. But he was going to have to apologize.

It was something he rarely needed to do.

The boy scouts had already eaten several of the fresh biscuits she'd made. A timer went off and she scurried to the oven with red mitts on both hands, pulling out a second tray.

"I've died and gone to heaven, Mimi. I expected someone would do a McDonald's run and if I was lucky, some Starbuck's, but this, this out of this world!" Joshua said in his thick Latino voice. He gave her a peck on the cheek.

"Why, thank you, kind sir!" she mimicked, patting him on the side of his left cheek with her red oven mitt.

She chanced a glance at Garrett who didn't try to stifle the smile that had bisected his face. Her eyes were firm and honest, unafraid. Garrett knew that her strength was just as attractive as the way she felt under his touch.

"Help yourself, Garrett," she challenged. "The plates are there, and these biscuits are only good steamy and hot." She followed the comment with a wink and he took all the meaning he could stand from it.

"Mimi, you're unbelievable. I never expected this,"

he said. "You're making my day."

"Good." She turned her back and dumped the hot tray into the sink, removed the red apron and then washed her hands.

She'd worn jeans and a red plaid flannel shirt. But she was barefoot with painted red toenails. She was back to putting her hair up, but this time wore a red bandana that tied in floppy red ears atop her head. He couldn't help but watch her hips as she sashayed to the side next to Luke, serving up some eggs and grabbing a hot biscuit.

"Oh man, they got jam!" Cornell said, rummaging through the refrigerator. "Feel like I'm back home in Mama's kitchen. Thanks, Mimi."

"Doing it for the team."

Fuzzy appeared in a fresh white tee shirt and scruffy khakis with loafers that had been worn over the heel so many times they became open-heeled slip-ons. "Mornin', everyone," he mumbled. He would not make eye contact with Garrett.

Everyone took seats around the kitchen on stools and chairs robbed from the dining room. The food was inhaled. Garrett took the last piece of bacon and made a mental note to have the boys get more.

Afterward, Mimi was inched out of the kitchen as the men helped with the cleanup. She managed to grab the trash bag and headed for the garage again. Garrett followed her.

"I always thought that was a two-person job," he heard Luke chuckle behind him.

She jumped when she turned and saw him standing there. "You scared me, Garrett!" Swiping her hands together, she washed them in the utility sink.

Garrett watched, not sure what he was going to say. The words were stuck in his throat. He'd acted like he wanted to tell her something he hadn't admitted he felt.

"I think I need to tell you I'm sorry about last night," he managed to push out before it became too awkward.

She didn't react. He was unsure what he expected but he wished she'd fill the space with some words. Perhaps everything had been a terrible mistake. He continued.

"I hope you didn't get offended with my behavior, what I did. I apologize if that was the case, Mimi." He was telling it straight from his heart, something he never did with a woman. He felt like a kid walking in his father's shoes that were six sizes bigger than his own feet.

"I had the same problem." She lowered her eyes. "Thought maybe you got the wrong impression of me. Maybe after this is all over with, we could do a reset, start all over like a couple of regular folks, not part of an elite stealth team looking to rescue a hostage? A very important hostage."

"I agree," he lied. His stomach churned. His hands ached to hold her again. He was thirsty for the taste of her mouth on his. He knew all this was wrong, yet he couldn't help but blurt out, "Can I have a raincheck, then?"

Her smile was beautiful, her opulent lips and smooth young skin screamed at him to lose control and blow the whole thing. But though his heart pounded, he needed to show her he could be trusted with his control.

"Of course. A raincheck, it is." As she slipped past him, she paused. "I'm not a slut, Garrett, and I don't sleep around."

He'd misread her. The sudden realization that he'd gotten overly anxious, that he'd done the very thing he promised himself he wouldn't do, flooded him with a combination of anger at himself and guilt. She was right. He'd let his feelings temporarily distract him from his mission. It was the same thing he'd given Fuzzy a hard time about.

"I never thought that about you, Mimi. Never crossed my mind."

She chuckled.

"I'm missing the joke," he said. They were close enough he could lean over and kiss her square on the mouth.

"My dad gave me the lecture about men. We used to have this old dog named Bruce."

"Sure, I remember Bruce. A real mongrel. Wouldn't stop fighting."

"Yes, that was Bruce. He never gave up, just like— you know what I mean. But Dad used to say to me, 'Mimi, boys are like dogs, like Bruce here. They get into a close encounter. Some fight, some go after girls, and then they move on to the next encounter. They don't think about it. They just do. It doesn't mean anything to them.' I forget that sometimes about men."

Garrett felt the vein in his neck pulse and his mouth go suddenly dry as he realized it was important what she thought of him. That never happened.

"Wait a minute Mimi. I totally get what you're saying, but that's not how I was feeling at all. I'm sorry you felt I was disrespecting you. Point taken. But don't go away thinking I just wanted a tussle in the sheets. That's not me. It upsets me that you think that way, too. I'll be totally hands-off. You can count on it."

Before he could hear her response, he abruptly turned on his heels and tore through the kitchen door. He joined the team in the kitchen and put his conversation with Mimi out of his mind.

After the cleanup was complete, the Special Agents Hoaglund and Desideri started coffee and dispersed it to the team, who had begun to gather around the dining table. They left with money and another list Garrett gave them.

Garrett stood by the large post-it sheet they'd stuck to the wall. He added comments from last night's texts under the motive label in one box. He saw Mimi check her phone.

"Anything?" he asked her.

She shook her head, no. Her expression was glum.

"Gents, we think Georgette tried to call Mimi last night from an unknown phone."

"She told me. That narrows our focus a bit. Good thing, too," said Joshua.

"Did she ask for help?" wondered Fuzzy.

"Yes. Sounds like she's being held." Garrett scanned the room again. Most had turned to watch Mimi, who was buried in her phone.

"I knew it," Fuzzy muttered. "Just didn't make sense she'd want to go on her own."

"I think it might have started that way, Fuzzy," Mimi quipped. "That's just a hunch."

"Could be all a planned false clue," said Luke.

"And she told us where she is," Joshua announced.

Garrett found himself a bit irritated. "She did. Oregon is what she said, at the POG farm."

"I can get a trace on that phone. Just make sure you let me know, day or night, Mimi," said Tanner, adjusting his glasses. "I'll need to check out the signal and perhaps trace the call through your phone." Garrett knew he would be calling his friend at Homeland Security.

He continued the discussion, laying out plans and giving assignments. "Time for a road trip. I've got to get this to Branson. I'm bringing the whole team, so let's get packing." Garrett knew the faster they could get to the compound the better.

"I'll call Mike with the update," said Tanner. "We're going to need some additional equipment. Someone's going to have to get in there to help with the surveillance."

Cornell Bigelow requested the floor. "I've got some specs on some listening devices we used on a private job. Really cool plugs that get shot strategically into a building. They have cameras and sound if they survive the blast and get planted correctly. Pretty damned cool. But not government issue. I got a source."

"You get on that, Bigelow. I'll get the money. The boys can do the pickup."

"Roger that." He ran to the next room, his cell phone to his ear.

"I better get started on the sewing," Tanner said, holding up a box. "I'll need a tee shirt from all of you, including you, Mimi. Gonna install some wires and tiny mics." Several small round devices and fine coils of wire were tightly packed in foam padding.

"Invisios. We got those?" asked Joshua.

"Branson sent them with the firepower yesterday. Glad to have them," answered Garrett.

"What's going to be the story? Someone's got to get inside, right? Make physical contact with Georgette?"

"That should be Mimi," said Fuzzy. "Someone should go inside with her. Perhaps they should pose as a couple trying to join the group, like say, her and Lopez here? You make a pretty cute couple." He winked at Joshua, and the men started catcalling and giving him a hard time.

Mimi studied Garrett's face. He saw the uncertainty there, even though she nodded and went along with the plan. Every few seconds, she examined her cell again, hoping for a text.

He left the group deep in discussion while he called Mike with the news of the contact. The pinging of Georgette's cell phone had not reoccurred. Mike also told him they came up with nothing on the table of youths at the breakfast.

"The president doesn't remember the POG representative. It was a woman, and he barely talked to her. He told me they'd made a six-figure donation to the first lady's favorite school meals charity. That's how they got the invite, through her. We don't often turn down the First Lady's requests."

"Either of them sense anything out of the ordinary?"

"They felt it was legit. I've had our guys look into the group, and nothing appears out of place. But I agree, you need eyes on the ground, now that she's asked for help."

Garret knew that if Georgette wanted to leave, she was in more danger.

"Mike, any chance someone on the staff is compromised?"

"Oh man, we're looking at that every minute. If that's the case, it's only a matter of time before we intercept them."

"But she's already gone."

"You tell me, Garrett. If she's being held against her will, do you think they don't know who she is? No. We think the president is being targeted through his daughter."

"Okay, well, get the arrangements made, and we'll take the next flight you can get," Garrett demanded. "I don't want to wait on this."

"I should be able to get you out there today. Just hold onto your hat and stay by that cell phone of Mimi's. Record those texts and get your gadget guy working on the tracing. Let me know if you need help."

"Thanks, Mike. Oh, and I almost forgot, any results from the prints on the book?"

"Nothing on file. There were two other sets of prints besides hers, but they were not known to the system. Afraid that's a dead end."

"Got it. Thanks."

"Garrett, there's one more thing. We got a reporter asking about where Georgette is. The FLOTUS told them it wasn't any of their business. I guess the reporter sort of took offense and is digging. This may not be a secret for very long."

"Just get us out there."

"Working on it yesterday."

Garrett's return to the team revealed Cornell had indeed secured the pop camera devices and the special agents would be returning with them shortly, which was welcome news. Tanner had collected the tee shirts. He sewed listening devices and tracking nodes inside pockets and underneath shirt logos, burying the wiring in the neckline and sleeve seams of the shirts. His work was flawless, undetectable.

"I'll need another two hours to finish. I can do it on the plane, if we got one," Tanner said.

"We do. Get your equipment tested and packed. Think we're leaving this afternoon," said Garrett.

Fuzzy waddled up to him. "Josh has done so much undercover work. I think he's our best bet for going in. You agree?"

Garrett's chest tightened. "I do."

"My suggestion is that Mimi change her appearance so she's not recognized, just in case someone knows about Georgette's teacher."

"How?" asked Mimi, who had overheard.

"I think you should change your hair color. Make it wild a bit, like you're someone who lives an alternative lifestyle," said Joshua. "I'll get the boys to get some colored shampoo that rinses out. Red would do, I think," he added with a wink.

"You up for that?" Garrett asked.

Mimi shrugged. "Anything. Whatever works."

He noted her defiance, trying to show her strength. It was a good attempt, but he saw right through it. He was certain she was terrified, now that the decision had been made. He was concerned about her, but wanted to keep his distance as he promised. He admired she didn't complain.

In less than two hours a large white van pulled up to the front of the complex. The drivers helped to load equipment. Mimi had just stepped from her room, drying her hair with a white towel that bled red. It completely changed her appearance, and made her look like a teen.

"You could pass for one of your kids," he smirked.

"Just my luck. I do something cool and 'with it' and everyone thinks I'm younger. You don't find it attractive?" She mimicked batting her eyes at him, which was so unfair.

"You know what I think, Mimi?" he asked, working on packing items in his Velcro pouches. "I already promised I'd keep my mouth shut, and a promise is a promise." He placed his hands on his hips to judge her reaction.

All he got was a pout and the slight rise of her eyebrows. If he'd allowed himself to react, he'd forget the talk and just kiss the hell out of her. But he knew it was better this way.

"Love it, sweetheart," Joshua said as he put his arm around her and gave her a kiss on the cheek. "Ready to go hippie?"

Garrett didn't like the fact that Joshua's arm remained over her shoulders and his fingers were too close to her ample chest.

Just before they left, he checked in with Branson and Mike.

The airstrip was an old private airport purchased by the FBI and used for special low-profile flights. The military transport was smaller than Garrett was used to being in, and the group had to huddle together since the strapped equipment took up so much space.

Mimi sat on the bench across from him, next to Joshua, who was giving her instructions about going under cover. With the plane droning on, it was hard for her to hear, and Garrett couldn't decipher a word, either.

He leaned back and resolved to get some sleep to make up for the lack of shuteye the night before.

Turbulence woke him up. He heard Cornell's headphones blaring next to him, but the man was oblivious, drooling over his own chin. Tanner was reading a book with a booklight clip. Everyone else was asleep or just relaxing. Mimi opened her eyes, and they stared at each other for several minutes before Garrett willed himself to close his lids and really try to rest.

It was easier, with the vision of her as the last thing he saw. Everything about her face was soft and not angry.

What the hell am I doing, getting her involved in this? He knew his worry about her safety wasn't all due to the fact that she was embarking on a mission for which she'd never been trained.

He snuck a peek, opening his eyes just enough so he could watch her again, and found that she was still studying his face.

His emotions were complicated, but it in a new and exciting way. There was something very satisfying about becoming her protector. He smiled and didn't care if she saw it.

CHAPTER 10

"**Y**OU HAVE TO think fast and be prepared for the unexpected. Watch your reactions, but if you get out of line, just go with it," Josh explained while they began the ride.

She knew it was easier said than done.

"Main thing is not to act scared, nervous, except for something your character would be scared or concerned about. Be wary of a good interrogator who's skilled at getting information from you while posing as your best friend. They can be watching you all the time, while you sleep, even in the shower."

"How many under cover missions have you been on, Josh?"

"No clue. Lost count years ago. I got so I forgot what city I was in, I'd been in so many drug operations. But with all that experience, I never let my guard down. You do that, and you might as well confess to be an imposter."

"Have you ever been kidnapped or shot?"

"A few. Had to rescue myself every one of those so as not to blow the mission. Truth is, if you need the outside to come in and take you out, it's usually too late. Be way ahead of them. Plan your escape. Start that day one, and then refine it every day so if you have to make a move, you're mentally prepared."

"Ever lost a hostage?" she asked.

Josh banged hit his head against the metal hull of the plane. "We don't think about those if we can help it. It's a dirty business. And some of the people I lived with I actually cared about. Maybe tried to get the innocents out, or help convert some of the bad guys. It's a risky and thankless job. But at least I never got bored. That would be the worst thing that could happen, Mimi."

She could imagine all sorts of things that would be worse.

"If one of the big guys comes on to you, try to keep out of it, but if you have to, be prepared to do what you have to."

"What does that mean?" she'd asked.

"Men and women, you know. Some men feel like they *own* women. We might have one of those here."

"You mean sleep with him?"

"I wouldn't call it that. It's something else. It's dirty and disgusting and should never happen to anyone, but be prepared, it might happen to you, Mimi."

"You think it will come to that? I mean, I'm a school teacher."

"I know, but the guy has a reputation. I've had to do some things in the field I couldn't tell my wife about. It comes with the job. Sucks, but that's what happens sometimes. I got friends who rode with bikers for years, took up wives and such. I want you to understand this before you go in. Are you okay with that?"

"I'm not going to hurt anyone. I won't do that for anybody. If I'm asked to do that, the answer will always be no," she said defiantly.

"I understand. I have the same issues. And some-times we have to prioritize the mission over our own welfare. It's what we did in the sandbox. But you do what you do to stay alive first, so you can help others. It's what police and fire and first responders do every day, Mimi. I hope it doesn't happen, but you got to be able to make that choice, should it come up."

She'd thought about that in the minutes before she finally found her sleep. She didn't understand how Garrett could be happy living in a cabin way out in the boonies after what he'd seen and done.

That's why there wasn't a woman in his life. He got bored easily.

THE BENCH SEAT was hard and Mimi woke up from an all-too-brief nap, disappointed she couldn't sleep. As she opened her eyes, Garrett's eyes peered deep into her soul, or at least that's how naked she felt. She inhaled, drawing strength from the extra oxygen, and stared right back at him without wavering.

She wondered if she'd been too harsh with him and regretted the mini-argument.

Within moments, he closed his eyes and appeared to go back to sleep. She studied his face. Without the beard, he'd have a firm jawline and smooth cheeks. His grey-blue eyes matched the silver streaks at his temples, giving him a distinguished look. She thought they'd gotten darker with age. As a child, she'd remembered their deep blue color, like gemstones of a rare quality.

When she saw his smile leak through, she worked not to smile back in return. She was sure it was meant for her, but just in case he was secretly watching her, or some other member of the team was onto the tension between them, she kept her face expressionless. It was hard to do. She knew the growing attraction for this man was slowly altering her whole world.

Garrett's arms were scared, and he'd covered over some of them with tats, just like her father had done. Her dad had even lost a joint on one of his little fingers in a battle he never talked about. Studying Garrett, she understood he had those same untouchable spaces that no woman would ever be able to penetrate. Men needed those secrets kept between each other in the arena. Her mother had understood that. And though she thought of his scars and tats as beautiful, she also knew that they were partially intended to be warning signs for any woman who might want to trespass. He was a true warrior.

She wondered again why he'd never married. He was legendary for some of his exploits with women, but unlike many of the other guys on the squad, he never landed a home and family. It seemed somehow sad.

Joshua's snoring was getting annoying, so she pushed him gently onto Fuzzy, who remained comatose. The Latino former SEAL had said a lot of things in preparation for their undercover caper and she hoped she would remember them all.

THE LANDING AT Eugene was hard, jerking her to attention. She stretched and yawned slowly, moving her neck and head, bending and straightening her legs to get rid of some of the kinks.

The blast of warmish fall air hit her face as the bays were opened and they were allowed to file out on portable steps. There was no covered gangway with carpet and nice music. Only a pair of young Navy pilots who shook their hands and wished them luck. To

Mimi, one of the pilots apologized for the hard landing.

They were quickly herded into black Suburbans with darkened windows and rushed off the tarmac. Garrett sat up front with their driver while Luke accompanied the second Suburban bringing Tanner and Fuzzy and a lot of Tanner's equipment.

She eavesdropped on the conversation between Garrett and the driver, Trevor, as they introduced themselves.

"You boys ever get inside his camp?" Garrett asked.

"Never really had reason to. Locals say they're not into drugs. Maybe a little pot, but nothing like before in Texas. We thought they'd finally settled down."

The driver was a huge black man, self-identified as a former drug counselor and occasional DEA driver, now working private security enhancement for law enforcement and FBI as needed.

"You look military, Hughes."

"No, sir, that's prison coding. And that's why I can't join the Bureau for real."

"You have a history then, I take it."

"That I do. My little brother was taken from me when I was serving my country—in a different kind of way. When I got out, I tried to get onto the force, join anyone who would have me. I don't qualify for anything, including being a janitor at a prison or shuffling paperwork for ICE."

Mimi's heart broke for Trevor's life circumstances. Garrett also was quiet and watched the road ahead of them. Blue mountains ringed the valley they were traversing.

"That where we're going?" He'd pointed to a set of foothills to the right.

"Exactly. They got a day lodge for you, and you're in luck, you've got power. All these were rebuilt after the fires and upgraded a bit. I think you even got mattresses, refrigerators and microwaves. But no heat. You gotsta chop your own wood for that."

Trevor's big body bounced with a deep chuckle that gave Mimi chills. She could see he liked to scare people.

"Have you ever met this pastor, Bales?"

"I saw him when I was working the fire line a few months back. Hard worker."

"So you think he's okay, then?"

"I didn't say that. I don't trust his ass. Something too clean and spiritual about him, you get my drift? Ain't nobody that perfect, I don't care how many times they try to show it. There's something off about him. But he sure is good with his flock. They love him. Especially the ladies." He followed up the comment with a wink, and then looked over his shoulder, noticing Mimi had been listening.

Garrett was next to notice her.

"I'd normally say this in private, but she's just his type," he said, pointing to her with the back of his thumb. "Miss fresh face there. You make sure she's ready, just in case."

They rode the rest of the way in silence.

Mimi found her stomach tied in knots by the time they approached the encampment. Along the long, winding road through the foothills, she remembered the pieces of advice Joshua gave her. Twice.

It didn't get any easier the second time.

CHAPTER 11

O N THE WAY from the airport, Garrett heard Mimi's cell ping. She dug it out of her purse and checked the screen.

"It's her."

He craned his neck so he could view the message. Joshua Lopez and others clustered around her. Tanner was on his cell, informing his contact at the Bureau. He nodded acknowledgement they'd started the trace and triangulation.

Help me.

"Ask if she can talk," Garrett instructed.

The answer came back, *No. Not safe.*

"Keep her texting as long as you can," Tanner whispered after he hung up his call.

Mimi handed the phone to him.

Tanner's fingers quickly asked a series of questions, including her specific location in the compound, and when she might be outside the gates.

They don't let me out anymore.

He also asked her if she was in danger. There was a pause before the response came through.

If I'm caught, yes. They know I want to leave. Can you get me out? What do I do to get out? Hurry.

Tanner texted back, *Still with Loren?*

Again, there was another pause, and then the answer, *Should not have trusted. Getting strange. Not safe. Want to leave. Mistake. Help me please. Hurry.*

"This is consistent with what I thought," barked Fuzzy Kinski.

Tanner asked her if she was hurt or injured in any way.

Not yet. But they tie up girls. Some beaten. Not safe.

Several of the men swore. Garrett made his right hand into a fist and then unflexed it several times.

Tanner tapped his ear buds, handing the phone back to Mimi. He stepped out of the Suburban first and walked to the side away from the crowd, in conversation. Garrett had asked him to find a used pickup and an older non-descript motor home they could use for listening, since they needed to be closer than the lodge. Garrett joined him.

Several agents began helping offload the equipment while Mimi and Garrett continued with the communication with Georgette. He helped her out so she could focus on her cell.

"Can I tell her we're coming?" she asked him. The wind had picked up and her firery red hair had come undone, bright strands flying in all directions. He was glad she was staying so calm.

"Do it. But don't say we're here. Ask her if she can hold on for a few days until we find out how to reach her."

Mimi nodded and sent the texts.

Thank God. I'll be praying.

Mimi texted back, *Is there anyone you can trust there?*

Maybe. Not sure. One of the brides I know.

"Brides?" Mimi asked.

"Ask her."

What do you mean brides?

Big ceremony on Sunday. Girls will be matched up. Not real wedding. I don't think I am. Not sure. I know someone who is. Can you help her too?

We'll try. What's her name?

Mallory. I know her from D.C.

From school? Mimi asked.

No. Just friend of Loren's.

Who is Loren?

Just a friend. I came with him and Mallory. Big mistake. But don't hurt him, OK? My father will send in the troops.

"Can't believe she's trying to protect him," Mimi scowled.

"He could be in on it or being used too," Garrett answered her. "Ask if there's to be any contact with POTUS."

Mimi nodded, typing, *Is this ransom? Will there be demands or communications coming soon? Do they know who you are?*

Not sure. Wanted to call them. Said to wait a few days. Then yesterday they told me I can't leave anymore. So I walked to the store and bought this phone.

Garrett was glad the girl had her wits about her. "She's smart. I'll give her that," he whispered.

"No, Garrett, not smart. Huge lapse in good judgment here. And some rebellion. That wasn't smart at all. I get that she's scared now."

Good girl. Stay calm. We're coming, but don't tell anyone. We're not here to hurt anyone but be ready, okay?

Okay.

Be brave. You can do this, Georgette.

I'm Greta. They call me Greta now.

You're Georgette and don't forget it, Mimi answered, biting her lower lip. *When can you call next? Can I call you?*

No, don't. I'll text when I can, maybe tonight.

Great job. Your mom and dad miss you. Just remember that.

After another pause, came the answer, *I miss them too. So sorry, Mimi. Tell them.*

NP.

The signal turned off. "Dammit, Garrett. What a mess this is. Do you suppose they targeted her, or her dad?"

"Doesn't matter. But good job staying cool. Time to insert. You ready?"

"I gotta go pee and maybe grab a sandwich or something. I have no clue what I'm doing, but I'm willing."

"Atta girl," he said, wrapping his arm around her

shoulders, hugging her close to his side. "You're doing great, Mimi. Really great."

She shrugged. "Yeah, they never prepared me for this in college. Never knew I needed to shoot and go undercover with a disguise."

"Hold on, there's not going to be any shooting unless we have to defend ourselves, or the innocents. Don't count on holding a gun."

"Now you're being smart. I'd probably shoot off my own foot!" she winked at him before starting to jog in place, then dance from side to side.

"Go pee, and I'll get you a sandwich."

He watched her follow a young agent to the hangar. Her nice pear-shaped ass would be a feature most people would miss due to her unnatural hair color, which made her look like her head was on fire. But Garrett didn't miss a single one of her moves as she disappeared into the building.

CHAPTER 12

MIMI AND JOSHUA Lopez hiked down the dusty road toward the People of God compound. Tanner had obtained the topo maps and pictures of the old compound when it was a terrorist training camp the joint task force shut down two years ago. They'd studied the terrain and the layout of the buildings that had been left behind. The satellite images hadn't downloaded as of the time they took off.

The plan was to get all the intel they could, make connections with Georgette, and then get out. Garrett had told her she'd be there for one day, two at the max.

The rest of the team hunkered down in an old Winnebago that looked like it had been rolled once or twice. But it ran, despite all the smoke it generated.

The pickup Garrett had purchased in town wasn't much better. It was a flat black two-door pickup with racks and yellow and orange flames painted from the rear wheel wells to the bumper.

Joshua checked his cell. "Damn, we only got one bar. I hope the reception is better at the top where the camp is. But I know they'll be able to hear us. I'd feel naked without the phone."

Mimi confirmed the same on hers. "And I got nothing from Georgette." She cleared the screen and replaced hers in a zipper pocket on the side of her backpack.

On any other day, the walk would have been pleasant. But today, she hadn't brought the correct shoes, wearing canvas tennis-styled lace-ups that hurt her big toe and cut into her ankle. That had been her fault, because she didn't prepare for the mission with a good set of shoes, even if they were new hiking boots. But, Garrett had made that snarky comment about her choice being perfect, which irritated her. That, and the reason for her visit was also anything but pleasant. So, this wasn't any old walk in the woods.

Damn him, anyway. He's not the one who's getting the blisters!

Joshua was talkative and appeared comfortable, which was both helpful and obnoxious at the same time. Mimi was always was more clear-headed when she was alone, or in the quiet, or with instrumental music that couldn't distract her thought process. But this was the situation she was dealt, and she worked to push aside her frustration because it would be just one more distraction.

She knew their entire conversation was being taped, so she tried to come up with things the team back at the base camp would have a chuckle over. They talked about good-fitting socks and underwear. They talked about movies, deodorant, and cars.

"You ever eat chocolate-covered crickets, Josh?"

"Let's see, I've eaten Mescal worms, snake, goat, and some beetles once in Mexico that gave me the runs, but no chocolate-covered anything, unless you're talking about body paint, and then, oh yeah, I've indulged!"

She wished she could watch their faces as they monitored.

"Remember to call me Carlos," he whispered.

"I keep forgetting."

"Just remember, curly Carlos," he said, wiggling his ponytail.

"You can remember mine because my panties are red today."

Joshua howled. "You get that, guys?" he murmured.

She scanned the sky. "No drones. Tanner thought there would be," Mimi said.

Josh put his finger up to his lips. He leaned into her. "I'm gonna tell you one more time to keep it strictly to the conversation we agreed on. You don't have to see or hear a drone to have them record everything you say," he whispered.

"So, Carlos, who are these people, exactly? How much religion do I have to tolerate? I haven't been to church since I was five and that left a lasting negative impression on me." She adopted their agreed-upon character.

"It's like they worship the land."

"Do they read the Bible?"

"I'd say yes. The pastor in charge used to have a church. Now he has a community."

"How old is this group?"

"No clue."

When they came upon a pickup parked by the side of the road, they added the planned demeanor of not getting along and her recent fight with her boyfriend back home. Josh thought it would be best if he was the one trying to convince her visiting the hippie commune would get her mind off her worries. And she was supposed to play being extremely stubborn.

Not exactly a difficult part for me.

While they examined the pickup, three girls and a young man materialized through the short scrubby bushes. One of the girls had long dreadlocks, which had attracted leaves and small twigs. All of their feet were covered in the dusty red clay soil residue. Unlike Mimi, they all wore hiking boots. The young male carried a bucket sloshing water and a fishing pole.

"*Hola!*" Joshua shouted, waving his hand.

The group displayed smiles, but the girls allowed their male companion to step toward them first.

"Greetings, friend. You here to receive the gifts of the land?" He held out his dirty and stained hand. "I'm Rocco."

He smelled of sweat and old fish parts. Rocco's hand was sticky with what she hoped was fish blood.

"I'm Carlos, and this here is Red," said Josh.

"Of course she is. Welcome. You just passing through, or are you on a real journey?"

Josh lobbed the answer right back at them, "We're seekers of the truth," while Mimi said, "Just passing through."

The four strangers laughed.

"We met up in town," Mimi started, her hands on her hips, brushing the sweat from her forehead with her forearm. "He invited me, but I'm taking the next truck I see heading back. As you can see, I'm not exactly prepared for this." She pointed to her dirty formerly white tennis shoes.

"Well, if you don't mind riding in back with the ladies, Carlos and I will drive you to camp. Maybe we can find someone there who can help with that request. Right, Carlos?" He winked at Josh and Mimi felt the deception beginning to work.

"Red, if you really don't want to stay, I'm sure they'll have someone who can take you back. I just thought it would be a welcome distraction." Josh added for the newcomer's benefit, "She just broke up with her boyfriend."

"Ah, I understand. We've got the right spot to start a new life," beamed Rocco, exposing a canine tooth that was missing.

Josh played the part perfectly. He helped her get into the truck bed where she took a seat with the other girls. It wasn't hard to act like she felt she was a fish out of water and about to enter a very dangerous game.

Mimi attempted to talk to the girls but couldn't hear over the sound of the truck motor. One of them lit up a joint, and they passed it around.

"Sometimes you have to make uncomfortable decisions when you're under cover. You want to be prepared for the unexpected."

She opted for truth when the joint came to her. "Hey, I've never smoked before. I'm not sure—"

The giggles from the ladies sounded like shards of broken glass falling around them. One of them coughed up their inhale and then spoke.

"You just take a little bit, see, like this. You *do* smoke cigarettes, don't you?" one of the girls asked.

"Nope. Never have." It was the truth.

"Okay, well, you're going to inhale a little bit, not

enough to be overwhelming to start. Just suck it in smoothly, like this." She demonstrated again. "Later, you'll learn how to take more in. Try it," she said, holding out the lumpy rolled paper thing Mimi was afraid to touch.

"I'm going to pass, sorry," Mimi said. "I get back to town I don't want to be smelling like pot. Just not my thing."

"It's completely legal now. Try it. You'll like it," said the girl with the dreadlocks.

"Thanks, but no." Mimi didn't want to appear too eager to fit in. But she also didn't want to introduce a new element into the mix and ingest something she'd never tried before. Even her former husband had wondered how she'd gotten through her young adulthood and not taken drugs. None of it appealed to her. She wasn't going to be afraid to show it, either.

That became the turning point. The group closed in to themselves and let it be known by whispering in a circle, their backs turned to her: Mimi—the strong-willed, red-headed newcomer—was an outsider.

THE ROAD UP the mountain was filled with ruts from fast-running water as they maneuvered around washouts and spun occasionally in gravel. Mimi's butt began to join the pain brigade along with her feet. She was parched as well. The ladies drank from their personalized water bottles, offering her sips as they cascaded up the mountain. Each bottle had their names painted on it, along with a bible verse and floral designs.

They approached the gated entrance. Concertina wire was coiled atop tall wire fencing she estimated at ten or twelve feet tall. High above, a guard station, manned by a muscled dark-skinned man holding a rifle, watched their every move. His mouth and nose were covered with a blue bandana.

A hand-painted sign hanging in a long arch above the gate had been skillfully lettered and adorned with crosses, pictures of healthy vegetables, flowers and praying hands. She read the words as the truck slowed to maneuver inside. The gates squeaked and appeared to have been forged from slabs of solid steel.

People of God,

Where All Good Shepherds Live Together In Harmony With Our Land.

Despite the sign, Mimi thought the compound still looked like a prison.

She scrambled out, rubbing her rear and trying to diffuse the pain all the bumping in the back had caused. She'd been seated partially on the wheel well.

"What do you think?" Josh asked. Their driver was standing next to him. A crowd had begun to gather to greet the newcomers.

She answered truthfully. "Carlos—and I mean you no offense, Rocco—I'm not impressed. What was I supposed to like about this dry, dusty place stuck in the middle of nowhere?"

She tried to say it loud enough so that, if Georgette were nearby, she might recognize her and know that they were coming to help.

A deep, rumbling voice boomed behind her. There was no question who was standing there. He was used to commanding a huge stage and did so, even in this dusty valley. Inside a building, he would have shaken the timbers.

"But you haven't seen God's bounty!" the voice said, rattling her eardrums.

Mimi turned and was shocked to see how distractingly handsome the pastor was. He sported a grin on his clean-shaven face, teeth blindingly white, with a turquoise earring in his left earlobe and a lush Navajo-style silver bracelet on his wrist. The pastor wore all blue denim and the most intricate pair of tooled and designed boots she'd ever seen. The rich brown leather was adorned with stitching and patterns enhanced by colorful painted designs.

His charisma was larger than the valley his community lived in. *No wonder he had followers,* she thought.

"I'm sorry. Forgive my lack of manners," the gentleman said. "I'm Nelson Bales, and who do I have the pleasure of welcoming to our little slice of Paradise?" He angled his head and gave her a wink, while his enormous paw extended.

Mimi allowed him to take her hand in his. He did all the shaking. Her inclination was usually to give as limp a handshake as possible when it came to meeting strange men, and this seemed the perfect time to continue that behavior.

"I'm Red. Nice to meet you," she answered him.

He was the sort of man who consumed the entire space around him. She felt his overbearing need for control and domination in a vibe enhanced by the fact that he didn't blink. As they talked, she found it necessary to pull away again and again, dropping her gaze.

"Red, what brings you here today?" he purred with his practiced velvet tongue.

"I'm reconsidering this at the moment. I bumped into this guy," she tried pointing to Carlos but couldn't find him. "He said you had a beautiful farm here I might like to see. I like gardening." She shrugged, hoping they wouldn't catch the lie.

"Oh, good. We have a fantastic farm here, feeding hundreds of people in the surrounding area."

"Yeah, he told me. I'm sorry, but if you have someone going back into town, I'd like a ride. I'm dirty, sore, and tired."

Rocco inserted himself into the conversation. "She's just broken up with her boyfriend, Brother Bales."

"So sorry, my child." His hand on her shoulder made her wince. "I can see you've been through a lot."

The man's feigned concern was downright creepy. All she could do was shrug. She wasn't lying about her desire to go back to the little town they'd come from.

"We'll discuss that later," said Bales. "Meanwhile, let's get you some food. And where is your companion?" Bales looked around him.

"Nice to meet you Pastor Bales," said Joshua, who inched his way through the crowd to shake his hand. "I'm Carlos. I hope you don't mind my inviting her. Truth is, I was on my way here anyhow and just thought this would be a good distraction for her. A chance to help her out."

Mimi made sure the harrumph she gave back was audible to the whole crowd.

"Sorry, sir. I'm afraid I misjudged her. Not the rugged type," he said as he rolled his eyes.

"Carlos, *all* are welcome! We heal what aches. Affairs of the heart are never easy." Bales boomed back at him. He addressed the crowd. "Come, come, let's be a family and show them some love. Let's prepare a small feast in our new friends' honor. Show them how we live and how we share!"

"Amen!" came the shout from the crowd.

"Please," he said as he extended his palm forward, showing the two of them the direction to walk.

The grounds were maintained spotlessly, small trails snaking through the complex bordered in smooth river stones the size of her fist. They'd been lovingly laid down then tapped into the soil to make a rounded definition of the trail. At the sides were raised beds abundant with flowers, colorful winter vegetables and fruit trees that had lost half their colorful leaves. Mimi noticed clusters of cabins, some surrounding a larger building in the center. There was a crudely built church with a steeple but no cross, and no bell. Someone was playing a piano inside the building.

"Where are you from, my sister?" he asked her, while he pranced at her side. They had gathered a small entourage of mostly young girls who followed like a cloud formation around a mountaintop.

"San Diego originally, but I've lived all over the place."

"That's a very fair city, if it wasn't for all the people."

"I agree."

"Are you in favor of what they've done to the islands and San Diego Harbor?"

"Boats, yes lots of boats. I get seasick easily, so I'm not a fan. I spent most my time looking at others surfing, walking the beach." It felt good to tell the truth.

"You go to church?"

"Not since I was a child," she lied. "I guess the beach was my church."

"And why was that?"

She stopped, suddenly stumped for what to say. It wouldn't be natural for a complete stranger to ask such personal questions nor would it be reasonable for her to answer them so willingly. She'd almost made a mistake and noted she needed to be careful. He was a skilled interrogator, like she'd been warned.

"I'd prefer not to say."

"Ah." He turned and began speaking to someone else and veered off to the side.

Several of the girls guided them to a large canvas tent with long rows of picnic tables beneath. Beyond, she could smell food cooking in the large hall that bordered the patio. Her stomach rumbled.

She turned back to find Carlos. "Smells good. I'm suddenly starved."

"Me too. This is lovely, isn't it, Red?"

"You're forgiven for now, but don't push your luck," she said as she smirked at him for the benefit of their audience.

"Ah, you'll forget about him in time. Just relax, hang out for a few hours and then we'll get someone to get you back. As for me? I like what I see. I think I'll stick around, if the pastor will have me."

Several young girls with flowers clipped in their hair brought fresh bread, steamed vegetables, and a cheese quiche. Nasturtiums and other bright edible flowers were tucked in and around their food.

Girls were everywhere. She noticed several were pregnant or towing youngsters by their suspenders. If there were more men, they were elsewhere, working in another location.

There were a few seconds when they were left alone. Josh leaned across the table and whispered, "Any better phone reception?"

Mimi unzipped the pocket enough to determine she had no reception at all. The screen was blank. "Nada."

"We got one other problem, too. Their security has some gang-bangers I recognize."

"Did they notice?"

"Dunno. I keep feeling eyes on my back, but that's not uncommon. How about Georgette?

"I've not seen her. But where are all the guys?"

"It's early."

Mimi saw a group approach them. "We have company," she warned.

"Brother Bales would like you to join us in the garden," said an older attractive woman of about forty. Her skin was well-tanned, and she wore dreadlocks.

"I'd like to see that," Mimi answered. "But could I take a peek at your kitchen first? I want to see the place where they prepared this miracle of a meal." She was hoping she could get a glimpse of Georgette somewhere inside.

The crowd smiled enthusiastically.

"Absolutely," the woman answered. "By the way, I'm Sister Jasmine."

"Nice to meet you, Sister Jasmine," said Josh as he stood. "And thanks for the food."

Sister Jasmine led them through a set of commercial double doors into the brightly lit warehouse-like kitchen.

The operation running before them was cranking out some serious food. Clusters of people, both men and women and even some children, were packaging bags of vegetables and flowers in brown paper bags with the logo of the commune on the side, beneath the words, *People of God Have Loving Hearts*.

"How many of these do you put together in a day?" Josh asked.

"Depends. Sometimes it can be as many as a hundred. But normally, we do less. Whatever the area needs, we're there."

Mimi guessed these were donation bags and not for sale. Several men were slicing fresh bread into generous slabs, making sandwiches, and wrapping them in plastic. The operation was a well-oiled assembly line of completely willing and happy workers who barely looked up.

Mimi was stunned at the scope of the operation. "Wow," was all she could muster. She shuffled her backpack, because one of the straps had dug into her shoulder and was getting painful.

"Let's get someone to help you with that." Jasmine reached toward her.

"I'm fine, really," she said, backing up to get away from her reach. She changed the subject quickly. "I just can't get over how much food I'm seeing."

"Pretty impressive, isn't it? We're rather proud. Wait until you see the gardens. It's even better," Sister Jasmine said with a knowing smile.

Before they exited, Mimi checked every face in the huge facility and found no evidence of Georgette. When they returned outside she also scanned the large gathering area in the center of the complex but still could not locate her. More men had descended into the complex, headed for the tented dining area.

Along the path to the gardens, Mimi made sure to comment on what she was seeing for the benefit of the team listening in. She asked questions about what they grew outside, what they grew in the large greenhouses she saw, and how they sent their things to market or to the donation sites.

"We have drop-off places all over Klamath Falls, and the little towns surrounding," Jasmine started to explain. "We also run a used clothing and furniture store right downtown in Klamath. No one is refused. Everything is sold cheap, but if someone cannot pay, we allow them to take what they want. The people here love our church."

"You must have a fleet of trucks to carry all this," Josh added.

"We do. We deliver once a day, occasionally twice."

Four long greenhouses sat in parallel rows at the edge of an enormous vegetable garden being tended by a dozen men and women. The fenced garden area was also planted in rows, by category, making the whole valley floor look like a giant variegated green-patterned quilt. The rust-colored soil was dark where it had been recently watered and worked into soft mulch around the plants. There were almost no weeds present.

"These four greenhouses are huge. What do you grow in there?" she asked.

"We do all our plant starts, cloning and some hydroponics—tomatoes are harvested year-round that way. And we grow herbs and other medicinal things." Jasmine grinned as Nelson Bales exited one of the greenhouses and waved to them.

"Sisters!" Bales called out across the yard.

"It's so beautifully organized. I think it's the nicest garden operation I've seen," Mimi exclaimed. She wasn't having to pretend. It was obvious the garden project was well planned and run by skilled nursery workers.

Bales spoke with two older, and well-muscled men before he broke off and came down the path to greet her. Josh was eating a carrot one of the girls pulled from the ground for him. All the women bowed their head to the pastor.

"We have big plans for this valley," he announced.

"I can see. Very impressive," Josh said between bites of carrot.

The pastor squinted, focusing on something on the other side of one of the greenhouses, and then addressed Josh.

"One never knows what can happen in the world today. We've got another forty acres on the other side of the creek we haven't touched yet. With all the political unrest, if we had to, I think we could feed the whole state of Oregon."

"I don't doubt it. You do all this with donations?" Mimi asked.

"Some sales, but yes, our work is blessed with rewards you wouldn't believe." He was studying her face, which made her feel uncomfortable.

"All volunteer labor, too. That helps," Josh said with a slight edge. Mimi wondered if the pastor would take offense.

"Not everyone understands. I think we are changing hearts and minds every day. Someday, people will understand how important our work is."

Several men approached them.

"Carlos, these men are going to show you to your quarters. That is, if you're staying?" Bales asked.

"I'd like to."

Mimi could see a wrinkle of worry cross his face. The pastor addressed her next.

"And Red, I've arranged for your accommodations as well."

"I was going to go back to town—"

"Just for the night." We've already completed our deliveries for the day." He held up his palm. "I'd like to personally invite you to the bonfire for our evening worship service. We sing, and like all hard-working chosen people, we go to bed early. We'll see to it you are returned tomorrow, if that is still your wish."

She looked across the group to Joshua, who was biting his lower lip.

"Well, I guess one night, then," she answered, knowing there was really no choice in the matter since they hadn't located Georgette. Josh was focused on watching several men on the perimeter of the garden, headed to the woods.

"Until tonight then. Ladies?" he bowed to Jasmine and the younger girls, who all lowered their eyes and their heads.

Josh was escorted in the opposite direction the girls directed Mimi to go. "So the men and women are separated?" she asked one of the girls.

"Sometimes. We do allow couples and family units, of course, but the single men are separated from the single women," answered Jasmine before a younger girl could respond. "It just works better that way. I'm sure you understand."

Her delivery reminded Mimi of some nuns she'd run across in school.

Mimi was joined by two new helpers, who brought three large baskets containing flowers and what appeared to be fresh clothes and a nightgown. She was shown to a small cabin where she could wash up and prepare for the evening service. Mimi was filled with questions but decided to just observe and not look too curious.

The little cabin had running water but no formal bathroom. It did come with a large soaking tub, which she was told could be filled with hot water heated by a hot spring cistern located beneath the site.

"The toilets are in that little row outside," Jasmine

pointed out. "If you require anything else, you can ring this little bell here and one of the girls will come to you."

Mimi examined the rusty bell by the front door. She also noticed that there was a lock on the *outside* of that door.

"What is this?" she asked.

"It's for your protection."

"Wouldn't I be more protected if the lock were on the inside where *I controlled* it?"

Jasmine gave her a patient smile. "Sometimes we get people joining us who have various *personal problems*. Pastor always says we don't always get the well ones. Or, unruly children who need a time out. Some days I think we all need a time out."

Two of the other girls nodded in agreement and giggled.

"Have no fear. No one will bother you. You're safe with us," she finished.

"We picked some flowers for you, Red," said one of the younger girls, placing the wide-mouth vase on the countertop next to the sink, highlighted by the dying sun's rays. The bright yellow baby sunflowers, snap-dragons, lupine and roses added country charm to the small space.

"Thank you. They're lovely," whispered Mimi.

A large crockery bowl full of apples and small winter pears was placed on her table, along with a small loaf of unsliced wheat bread, some butter and a knife. A covered pitcher of water and a clean glass were set nearby. Towels and the nightgown were placed on the bed. One of the girls lit an oil lamp and set it beside the flowers.

"Bring the lamp with you when you hear the call to worship, so you can find your way there and back," Jasmine said.

"No electricity?" Mimi was wondering how she'd keep her cell phone charged.

"I'm afraid no, not in this cabin. We're running out of space; we're expanding so fast! It's a good problem to have, don't you think? Way better than in a noisy dorm with ten other women. You'll be comfortable and warm enough here."

"When is the service?"

"An hour after nightfall. You'll smell the bonfire, see the light and hear the bell. I'll have Sister Rebekah meet you outside to help guide you. But bring your lamp so you can see the path."

"Thank you."

"Of course. You want me to draw your bath water?"

"No, if it's just turning a fawcett, I can do that." Mimi lowered her backpack on what appeared to be a very comfortable bed covered in quilts. "I think I'll try a soak. I'm sure I have blisters," she said, pointing to her tennis shoes.

"I'm sorry. I think there's some salve in the cupboard over the sink. We keep it for the garden workers and for bee stings and mosquitos."

"I have something. But thanks."

"My pleasure. I leave you now. See you in about two hours then?"

"I'll be right outside after the bell rings," added Rebekah.

"Thank you," said Mimi. "Jasmine, where do you stay?"

She smiled, tying her dreadlocks back with a piece of frayed ribbon. "Why, I stay with my husband, of course. Pastor Bales, dear."

CHAPTER 13

G ARRETT THREW DOWN his headphones.
  "Goddammit!"

Tanner and Fuzzy remained seated. Fuzzy spoke up first.

"You don't know for sure they blew him, Garrett."

Outside the van, Garrett could see Cornell Bigelow throwing rocks, aiming at stacks of flat pebbles he'd placed on boulders hugging a small creek. Every sharpshooter he knew liked to skip stones or toss pebbles to hone their craft when they had spare time. It was a nervous habit he had as well.

Garrett was angry with himself that he'd let Joshua accompany her. And now something wasn't adding up right.

Fuzzy, Luke and Tanner all waited for him to give them direction.

"Joshua's very intuitive. If he wasn't certain they hadn't made him as ex-DEA, then we gotta worry about it," he grumbled, crossing and uncrossing his arms while he watched Cornell.

"You couldn't have known, Tierney," added Luke.

"I should have guessed it, though. Our guys tipped us off there would be weed. I should have thought of it first."

Tanner was still attempting to listen, but it had been nearly an hour since Josh's wire stopped working. Lopez hadn't given them any warning. He just stopped talking.

"Is there a signal?"

"Oh yeah, it's there. But the fuzz I'm getting is like white noise. I don't hear any muffled voices at all, Garrett."

Bigelow came inside, grabbed a water, and sat down cross-legged on the floor beside Tanner, waiting for instructions. Mounted over the couch behind the former SEAL was the sign *What Happens in The Camper, Stays in The Camper.*

Tanner whispered something to him, and Bigelow nodded back.

"Do we all go in, then?" asked Luke.

"Not until someone tells me Georgette is there and, hopefully, is in good enough condition to be rescued. Mimi seems to be fine, but I've got to warn her."

"You?" asked Fuzzy. "Why not one of us?"

Garrett didn't want to have to explain something

he couldn't explain. He'd never forgive himself if something happened to Mimi. But he knew the most dangerous place to be was *inside* the camp if a raid was called, and he needed to be there to protect her, if necessary. He didn't want one of his men to take that risk.

It took him all of thirty seconds to decide. He couldn't spend any more time thinking about it. Time to get into action. He began to bark orders, just like he did when he ran platoons on the teams.

"I need Bigelow to come with me, to find good position and cover us. I need you on the com, Tanner. Your eyes and ears, too, Fuzzy, to help assess what's happening if it turns out to be a full-scale hostage rescue. If something happens to me, you've got to signal Cornell here, and Tanner, you'll have to call out for more help. And, Luke, we might need your kit. So, there you have it. And just in case I wasn't clear, nobody sleeps until we get them all back safe, understood?"

"You gotta wear an Invisio, Garrett. You both do," Tanner said, pointing to Bigelow. "I gotta be able to talk to you."

"Absolutely. Was counting on that. And get hold of Mike, too. I need to know if there are going to be any news media issues. You can talk to me while we're hiking up there."

"Roger that. So, you're leaving now?"

"Like yesterday."

It was funny. The more dangerous things got the more comfortable he felt. He'd brought along an old backpack, stuffing his clothes and his extra clips inside. He pulled out a sleeveless motorcycle tee, yanking it over his head. The pinup girl design on the backside would be hard to miss. Then he changed into a pair of old jeans with holes in the knees and a stain spilled on the thighs. He also wrapped a dark blue and white checkered headdress around his head and neck. He'd picked it up in one of the village markets and wore it overseas for years. He felt it brought him good luck.

Slipping on his black, lightweight Kevlar mesh jacket, he hoisted his pack over his shoulders and adjusted night vision goggles around his neck. Cornell was in all black, his duty bag twice the size of Garrett's, with enough firepower and grenades to start a small war.

Tanner handed them the tiny earpieces which they both inserted as deeply into their ears as they dared and checked for sound. When Tanner gave them the thumbs-up, they were out the door, readying for the high-speed mile run to the outskirts of the camp.

Garrett was ten years older than his sharpshooter teammate, but he wasn't going to go easy on the man. He knew Bigelow had set sprint records at BUD/S and, from the size of him, kept himself in marathon condition. It was time to make a point. He loved testing himself to extremes.

The first part of the trek was fairly level, but as the darkness descended on the hillside, the trail got thin, then disappeared into the brush. They flipped on their NV goggles, but barely slowed down. Luckily, there wasn't a full moon, so no flash came off the moonlight dancing on rock formations to blind them.

Garrett got the message that Mike had pulled a favor and got the nosey reporter stopped, which was a relief. DHS was still checking White House staffers. And there was no further activity on Georgette's old cell phone or computer.

He turned, looking over his shoulder, and found Bigelow keeping one pace behind him, hugging his ass just enough to let him know there was no way he was going to let an "old guy" beat him.

As they neared the crest, the terrain leveled out again and he could feel the cool breeze coming from a verdant plateau. The temperature had dropped as well.

A glow from a bonfire made the trees in the foreground look like they were on fire and interfered with their night vision. Garrett slipped his backpack around his neck and sniffed the crisp air laced with the scent of fire.

Carefully maneuvering around large boulders, they

found a gathering of more than a hundred men, women, and children all holding hands, singing in unison. After several stanzas, the group would stop, and as Garrett listened carefully, he could hear one male voice addressing the crowd.

Cornell touched him on the shoulder and pointed to his left. Several hundred yards away were four greenhouses lit up from within. At a considerable distance from the compound itself was a large hangar-like structure. They could barely see long vertical and horizontal lines of incandescent light escaping from what appeared to be huge doors. He removed his camera and sent a picture to Tanner.

"Not sure Mimi saw this, so see if we can get some satellite image in the morning, Tanner."

"Affirmative."

Garrett used his small binoculars, surveying the scene. "Gathering, maybe more than a hundred, some children too. I don't see—wait! I see Mimi there. Thank God for the red hair."

He held up his cell again, enlarged the view, and attempted to get a picture, but felt his hands shaking. He inhaled several times and felt better.

"Sorry, gotta wait until I catch my breath."

Cornell shook his head. Garrett tried again and snapped the shot, sending the image on. Digital numbers reflecting distance to the edge of the crowd would show up on the image. Their tracking would enable Tanner to pinpoint exactly where they were on the topo map and pass it up the line if necessary.

"No doubt about it. Red's a good color on her, Garrett," came Tanner's voice in his earpiece. "She actually has a decent voice, too."

Garrett studied the crowd but didn't find Joshua anywhere within it. "No sign of Lopez," he whispered.

"Copy. I still have a signal that hasn't moved, but no voice patterns."

Garrett swore. "We're gonna get set up. I see some security on the periphery. Seven, eight, nine, twelve, and maybe more."

"Copy."

Both he and Cornell changed their focus away from the bonfire, surveying the dark shadows dancing amongst the boulders beyond. They were alert to any activity outside the fire circle and noted the tall lookout bucket atop the entrance, which had been left open. At the current time, the guard shack appeared abandoned.

"Wish I could have that spot," muttered Cornell.

"Yeah, and you'd be a sitting duck when the shooting starts." Garrett handed him his binoculars. "Take a look up that little swale. I see a huge oak tree. And you got your rocks behind it, so I think it would be good cover if you can see everything."

Cornell checked the spot out and agreed. "Showtime. I'll let you know when I'm in position. Gonna go the long way around, but hell, I'm ten years younger than you, old Bone Frog, so I can make it no problem."

"And you probably won't get winded either, you asshole."

"Sucks to be old."

Even in the dark of night, Garrett could make out the stark white grin from Cornell's teeth.

"Keep your head down, brother." Garrett's sendoff was barely a whisper.

After a few yards, Cornell, with his duty bag strapped to his back, disappeared into the brush without a sound. Garrett went back to watching the group holding hands and singing.

He identified Nelson Bales easily both because of his height and the white robe he wore. When the music stopped, several youths stepped forward and he laid hands on their foreheads in a blessing.

Adjusting his gaze, he found Mimi and brought her face into focus, enlarging it. Her eyes darted from side to side, and she looked nervous as hell. She wore a baggy pair of overalls, with the peasant shirt that had the microphone Tanner had sewn into the seam. Her hair was pulled up in one of her clips, the edges looking wet.

Garrett scanned the crowd just as she did, looking for Georgette or Joshua, but found neither. There was no smile on Mimi's face as she continued what he knew was a desperate search for something familiar. He could tell she was reaching the edges of what she could tolerate.

Hang on there.

"I'm in place," came the message from Cornell.

"Copy. Waiting for the crowd to disperse. I'll message when I begin to initiate contact."

"I'm seeing a small building with bars on it. They've got a posted sentry. I'm thinking Josh," came Cornell's voice in his ear.

"That will be next on the list.

CHAPTER 14

IT FELT JUST like Halloween. Shadows lurked, bonfires raged, and secret rituals were followed. Something was waiting to jump out at her when she'd least expect it. It was like Mimi had gotten stranded with a bad date and the wrong crowd—a dangerous crowd. Or one of those days when she shopped for clothes and nothing fit. *Somewhere* there was a place where she belonged, but this was not it.

People were milling around after the songfest, greeting each other, laughing, and some walking arm in arm. The bursts of fire from the huge pit made the trees surrounding the clearing dance like they were ancient Native American spirits with evil intentions. She listened to fragments of conversation, unsure where she should stand or even where she should head next. She gripped her gas-fueled lamp and waited, turning slowly like a lost child.

Under the glow of firelight, people's faces looked

grotesque and unkind. She much preferred the soft, innocent-looking pastels of early morning or afternoon light. Mimi was all alone and didn't trust anyone enough to ask questions about where Joshua had gone or even how to get back to her cabin.

Until Nelson Bales approached. He'd been studying her from across the clearing for some time, he said.

"I can see you're uncomfortable, sister." The wildness in his eyes made her defensive.

"Is it that obvious? I don't know a soul. Did Carlos ditch me?"

He watched her closely—too closely. "What makes you say that?"

She shrugged. "I just thought he'd be here, that's all."

Bales paused. "How well to you know him?"

He was the skilled negotiator like Joshua had warned her.

"I don't. Like you, I've just met him."

Mimi tried not to look at up, so eyed people as they passed by. Nelson Bales carefully placed his palm on her shoulder, which made her jump.

"Do not be afraid, little one. I'm here to protect you."

This had the opposite effect on Mimi. Her blood pressure spiked. She immediately stepped back and crossed her arms.

"Please don't do that." She held up the lantern in front of her, making it become a barrier between their two bodies.

"I apologize."

"So where did he run off to? Can you tell me, then?"

"We're making arrangements for his stay. He's still here."

Mimi didn't like his non-answer but didn't want to ask any further. "Your wife told me you were at capacity. I'm sorry we've imposed on you."

"All are welcome, as I've said before. Come, I'll have Rebekah take you back to your cabin, so you can get a good night's rest, and then we'll talk more in the morning."

He motioned for the young girl to approach. Mimi thought she caught a glimpse of Georgette standing with a young man near one of the trucks, but when she looked closer, they had disappeared.

"Until tomorrow, sister." He bowed and then retreated into the night. She was glad there was distance between them.

Her guide walked forward, nodding in the direction they would be traveling. Mimi kept pace right alongside her.

"How long have you been here, Rebekah?"

"Nearly a year now."

"You like it?"

"Oh yes! I'm hoping Pastor Bales selects a good husband for me soon."

"A husband? *He* picks your husband?"

"That's the way it's done here at POG. We serve until we're called. I admit it took some getting used to at first, seeing the marriage ceremonies, but people are happy with the arrangement."

"Sounds very archaic." Mimi was working hard to keep her voice from cracking. She also resisted the urge to just run as fast as she could for the entrance.

"Surely you know it's been this way for centuries all over the world."

"Doesn't anyone ever protest?"

"Those who are too difficult leave. We don't want them here."

A group of children ran across their path, nearly colliding with the two of them. She watched them disappear and continued investigating the shadows for any familiar face she could recognize. Again, she found none.

Rebekah said good night, giving her a hug, and they parted at the front door to Mimi's quarters.

Inside, she sank to the bed and put her head in her hands. Slow hot tears fell on her chest just from the sheer overwhelm of events. It had been a very long day. They'd flown out from the east coast, traded texts with

Georgette, wormed their way inside the camp, and then she'd been abandoned. Her cell no longer worked, and she wasn't sure the microphone in her shirt was still communicating, either. There was no sign of Georgette. It was dark, and she was alone, completely alone, in a one-room cabin she was unable to secure.

She took several deep breaths, listening to the sounds of the night. Then she slowly rose, walked to the table and grabbed an apple and glass of delicious water. As she studied the walls and noticed the beautiful cotton quilts hung over the bedframe and over the bed itself, she felt like she'd stepped back in time. It was like she was traveling on an untethered adventure, playing a role she'd never played before, doing things totally unfamiliar. Everything she was used to had been stripped away. Even her new friends responsible for her safety were too far away to help if she had the need.

Mimi placed the apple core in a paper bag lining a basket by the kitchen sink. It had done little to calm her stomach or her nerves. She washed her hands in hardwater lavender soap, rinsed, and then removed her flip-flops carefully so she wouldn't disturb the large blisters that had formed on her heels and big toes. Her overalls fell to the floor easily. She slipped her night-gown over her head, leaving her shirt on underneath because of the cold, but also just in case the little device was still sending a signal back to the base. After turning off the lamp, she tucked herself into bed, pulled the quilts up to her chin, and prepared to sleep.

But sleep was elusive. Occasionally, voices and animal sounds from outside broke through the night, including the howl of a wolf. And then it got very quiet.

What was she doing with her life? She missed everything that made her feel happy and secure. Mimi let the sadness wash over her, not fighting the tears dripping from the corners of her eyes into her hairline. She knew she'd be up all night, clutching the covers, shivering in the cold until her mattress warmed up. She was a ten-year-old child again with no one to protect her.

She vowed that when she managed to escape from this little Hollywood horror movie she'd quit running away from things and begin running toward something beautiful.

Mimi lost track of time. An hour or more went by until she thought she heard someone outside her door. She sat up then padded quietly to the table and grabbed the dull knife, ready to defend herself. She couldn't see the doorway but did hear the latch on the metal handle being turned very slowly and deliberately. Her heart raced as she prepared herself for the worst, considering all the tools she had to use. There were the two chairs and the huge crockery bowl or the heavy glass pitcher.

She could even throw the covers over someone if she had to.

A burst of cold air blew into the room, and a hulking figure obscured the view of the bright stars outside. She remained very still, slouching in the corner, waiting for her visitor to come looking for her in bed. Then she'd pounce.

"Mimi? Are you there?" came the whisper, unmistakably Garrett's voice.

Relief flooded over her entire body as she realized he'd come for her.

"Oh, Garrett!" she sighed, running straight towards him, slamming up against his chest and feeling his arms encircle her. She pressed herself into his hard body and began to shake.

"It's okay, Mimi," he said as his big hands sifted through her hair. "You're doing great, sweetheart, just great."

"No. I'm. Not. I don't want to be here, Garrett. I want to go home. I don't belong—"

"Shh, shh. Don't say that. Have you found Joshua? Any idea where he is?"

"Bales said he was still here. I think they're holding him somewhere."

"I have a hunch. But you've not seen him?"

"No." She began to shake again. "I think I saw Georgette, though."

"Good." He rubbed his hands up and down her spine, then massaged the muscles at her upper neck. "Better?"

"Garrett, I can't do this any longer. You need to get me out."

"Quiet, Mimi. We have to be very careful not to get discovered," he said, holding her face between his giant palms. His thumbs rubbed away her tears. "Don't be afraid, honey."

He kissed her eyes and cheeks, and then his lips were brushing against hers.

"Please, Garrett, get me out of here. I can't do this!" she said between kisses.

"You can. I wouldn't have asked you if I thought you couldn't do it. Help is on the way. You're not alone."

She didn't want to hear that and began to pull away, but he held her tighter, refusing to let go. She pressed her palms against his concrete chest, but he still hung on. She twisted to the side and tried to wiggle free but found it impossible.

"Mimi, stop it. Calm down. You're alright. Everything's going to be fine."

"No, I don't want to do this. Get me out of here," she insisted.

But Garrett would not let her go. She could feel tension in his powerful arms, in his hands that gripped her tight.

"Mimi! Stop it!" It was a whisper, but it was a command.

She stopped just long enough to reset her emotions, gulping in air and trying to stop her shaking. She began to notice the rhythm of his heavy breathing, long and slow, matching hers. She could feel his anger brewing or his disappointment.

He released her and stepped back.

"I'm so sorry," he whispered. She could barely hear him.

"Garrett, I'm just not good enough. I wasn't made for this, like you were."

Although she couldn't see him, she felt his body heat and the gentle touch of his hands at her shoulders, smoothing up her neck and angling her face up towards him. He caressed her hair with his strong fingers but left the hot space between them without kissing her again.

"Don't tell yourself that, Mimi. It isn't true. You are strong. In fact, you're one of the strongest women I know."

She didn't move, loving the warmth of his palms, the sounds of his voice, and the feel of his chest rising and falling. At last, he'd traversed the distance and his lips nibbled at hers.

"You're fearless," he continued, deepening the kiss

afterwards. "Intuitive," he murmured, kissing her again. "So smart." His lips brushed back and forth across her hungry mouth. "You care about people and that's what makes you so strong."

She took a deep breath, readying herself for what she hoped was coming next, allowing the warmth traveling down her spine to set her insides on fire with a deep craving for his touch.

And then his lips were there, consuming hers and begging her to open up to him. The fire in her belly grew, settling her shaking but leaving her breathless. She was starved for his kisses, melting into his hot body. His muscled arm wrapped around her waist, pressing his groin into hers deliciously, showing her his need.

"Garrett—"

He gently put his palm against her mouth to stop her. "Shhh," he whispered to her ear. "You're wearing a wire."

Damn it.

But the wheels were already in motion, and she was unable to stop. Instead, she quickly pulled her gown over her head, allowing her thighs to brush against the rough denim of his jeans. She stood close enough to feel the length of him against her as she removed her shirt and tossed it into the corner far away. Her nipples knotted up as she stood in front of him completely naked and wished he could see her. Her palms slipped over his chest, up to his neck as she pressed her breasts to him, and felt his quick inhale.

He picked her up and carried her over to the bed, placing her gently on top of the covers. She heard the mechanical sound of something metal being carefully placed on the ground and then the friction of material as his clothes dropped to the floor. In seconds, his powerful body was on top of hers, his hips writhing against her, rooting to find her opening. His hands squeezed her breasts as he bit and kissed her neck under her right ear. He slid his palms beneath her rear, raising her pelvis up to angle for him. Her knees fell to the sides. His cock brushed back and forth against her lips.

"Mimi, tell me to stop and I will, sweetheart."

"No. I don't want you to. I need you inside me, Garrett. Please," she begged, arching her spine and pressing his buttocks down as he thrust up and deep inside her.

They blended into one another in a dance of muscle, strength, and tenderness. His powerful hips pushed him to the hilt and sent her into oblivion as he repeated his motion over and over again, pressing against her internal walls, stoking her fire.

He stretched her arms over her head and held her wrists together with one hand, using his other to lift her pelvis to accept him, going deeper with his slow rocking motions. The more he kissed, touched, and squeezed her body, the more she needed him.

Their lovemaking was urgent, but Garrett was patient, pausing several times to let her feel the power of her own orgasm before slowly rebuilding the rising tide of desire so that she could experience it all over again and then flutter back down to earth. He was attentive, careful, but loved full out, with complete abandon.

He left her feeling like a rag doll, soaking wet and completely out of breath as she felt his long release.

Neither one of them spoke. Her fingers drifted up and down his powerful back, traveling over his rear and down the backsides of his thighs. She traced the arc of his ear and kissed him tenderly there.

"Stay. Stay with me. Don't go."

"In due time. But I can't stay tonight."

The black of night started to give way to a dark grey promise of morning. Her eyes began to see his jawline and handsome face.

With arms and legs tangled, she was lulled to sleep, exhausted, curled up in his arms that still held her body tight as if he could squeeze away all her fear and make her fly.

Minutes later, he woke her with probing fingers and wet kisses and quietly slipped out of bed.

"Don't."

"I have to, Mimi."

She sat up and watched him dress. "Stay a little longer."

"Honey, it isn't safe. But you can count on me showing up tomorrow—rather, today. In the meantime, wear your shirt—" He handed it to her.

"Does it work?"

"We heard it all, sweetheart. And I'm sure Tanner's gotten an earful tonight." His long fingers touched her lips, making a line down between her breasts, ending up at her belly button. She accepted the shirt and loved the feel of him dressing her. His scarred hands smoothed down her thighs, his eyes following their travel. "You have such a beautiful body, Mimi. You're perfect."

It was the first time a man had ever said that to her.

She teared up, grabbed his hand and kissed his palm. "I want these fingers to touch every inch of my body. I want to do this all night long."

"We will. I promise. I keep my promises, Mimi."

She sensed he had something difficult to share with her. "What is it, Garrett?"

"I realize now we haven't much time. I can't leave you here for very long. You've got to find Georgette. Can you do that for me?"

"I will. I'll scout around this morning. I know she must be here somewhere. What about Joshua?"

"I think I saw where he could be held."

He pressed her back down onto the mattress and rolled her on her side, tucking the covers up over her shoulder.

"Rest up, a few minutes, Mimi. Today's a big day," he said as he kissed her cheek before he left as quietly as he'd entered.

Basking in the glow of what they'd shared, she no longer shook. She dreamt of blue waves and white beaches and Garrett running to her, carrying his surfboard tucked under his right arm.

CHAPTER 15

THE MOTORHOME WAS completely quiet when Garrett and Cornell returned. Everyone was still up, but no one wanted to make eye contact. It was nearly dawn.

"I'm going to get a little shut eye for about an hour, and then we'll go back and get her, get them all. I think I discovered where they're holding Josh."

"What about Georgette?"

He shook his head. "Mimi said she thought she saw her. She's going to look this morning." He finally made eye contact with Tanner. "You heard—?"

"I heard it all Garrett. I liked that part about your fingers all over her body," he said with a smirk.

Everyone chuckled.

Fuck.

Luke's smooth voice cut through the laughter. "You better keep that promise, Garrett. She's never going to let you forget it, either." He winked.

"We're witnesses," barked Fuzzy. "You lucky dog."

"Okay, I deserve all this and more. Rest up if you need it. Then everyone but Tanner goes in."

"I'm waiting for satellite images any minute, Garrett," began Tanner. "They're setting up the live feed as well. So I'll catch you on the other side of your power nap."

"That'd be nice. Everyone else, try to get a quick rest."

Garrett crawled to the rear bedroom and was out before he felt his head hit the pillow.

FUZZY WOKE HIM up. "Showtime."

Garrett threw cold water on his face and brushed his teeth. Then he grabbed several power bars, placing them in the used backpack they'd bought in town. He downed the meal replacement shake Cornell handed him. He tucked his Glock into the waistband of his jeans at the small of his back and secured the clips he'd brought, zipping them into a side pocket on the canvas backpack. He'd already switched out his underwear, and decided against shaving, and laced up his boots.

Fuzzy and Luke checked their weapons and tested their Invisios, as well as the wires Tanner had sewn into their shirts, making sure their Kevlar vests didn't interfere with reception.

"DHS is on standby in case you need more boots.

They can deliver within four hours of the call. And they have two birds they're grounding as backup in an emergency, just like you requested."

"Sweet," muttered Garrett. "We never got that kind of service overseas. I must be a big shot now."

"And here's the sat photo." Tanner laid out several black and white prints of the compound and the surrounding area.

"That's where I think they're holding Josh," Garrett pointed. "This building over here I'd sure like to get a look at." He put his finger on the long warehouse beyond the greenhouses he'd seen last night. "Cornell, you make sure you can cover us there from your perch."

"Roger that. Won't be a problem, sir."

"Here's where Mimi is." Then he brushed over the terrain above the encampment. "Tanner, you watch for activity here. Make sure they keep the link open 'cause you're our eyes. Lots of off-road trails, and now that I look at this, I can see they're well-traveled. They also have a second entrance at the back beyond the gardens. We're going to have to block that if we need containment. I also don't want reinforcements coming in and giving us a surprise party, understood? So you report any vehicle movement, especially a convoy."

"Hell, yes, I'm on it. Garrett, I also got some good smoke-belching drones in case we need them."

Cornell pointed to a ridge of trees. "I'll be up there, like before, except inside the perimeter this time with y'all. You tell me when the party's started, Tierney."

Garrett pointed to the dozen larger buildings. "We got a lot of places to check for Georgette. She could be anywhere. Tanner, if Mimi finds anything, she'll let you know."

He let the group study the pictures for a few seconds.

"Last minute questions?"

"Give us the code on the use of force, Tierney," barked Fuzzy.

"We're the Bone Frog Command, and as I told you back in Virginia, we're here to get in and out without too much fanfare, but if we have to stir things up, we do it. Deadly force is used only to save the life of an innocent or one of our team members. But you better be damn sure. We're just here for the girls and Josh. We let the locals clean up the illegal crap they might be engaged in. Drugs probably. And with all the rumors, maybe trafficking girls. But until we see proof, that's not our job. Understood?"

"Let's rock-n-roll," said Cornell.

Before they left the motor home, Garrett gave one last instruction to Tanner. "You hear anything about Josh or hear from him, or find out the signal's moved or stopped, you make sure I know about it right away."

"Roger that."

The team began the jog up the slope to the camp. Garrett slowed for a quick rest for Fuzzy's benefit. The tough cop was keeping up, but his face had already turned bright red, and Garrett could see he was stressed.

"Got about twenty more minutes, Fuzzy. Piece of cake, right?"

He got a finger for the comment while Fuzzy poured water on his face and then drank the rest of his bottle. "You just worry about yourself, old man. I'll be fine."

They heard trucks in the distance so the men moved into the brush a few hundred yards from the enclave entrance. Three covered trucks with the People of God logo ground their gears and made their way slowly past them down the hill.

"Looks like deliveries have started," said Luke.

When they came to the perimeter fencing, Cornell tested it first and then cut a square in the wire large enough for even Fuzzy to get through. One by one, they crawled on their bellies and then ran between boulders, brush and small saplings for cover. Garrett gathered the team together first before giving assignments.

"You know the passwords?"

Everyone nodded.

Cornell signaled and disappeared into the brush to take up his sniper position.

Garrett used his scope to assess the activity of the camp. He saw people milling about a large canvas tent. The smell of fresh coffee and cooking food permeated the air.

He handed his single scope and binoculars to Luke. "I don't want them to find this, but I'll take my chances with the Glock. Keep checking for our people. I'm headed for the entrance."

"I'm in position," Cornell's voice came over the Invisio.

"Can you shoot a couple of those darts into the building with Joshua?"

"You got it."

He heard the faint tinkle of breaking glass. "Tanner, can you confirm?" asked Garrett.

"Oh yeah, that's him. He just gave me a ton of attitude in Spanish."

"That's good news." Garrett faced Fuzzy and Luke. "So I'm going back outside. You guys find cover where you have a clear view of the entrance. I'm going to go pick a fight. We get Josh, find the girls, and get out of this place, quick. Understood?"

"Be safe, brother," whispered Fuzzy. Luke gave him a salute.

Garrett wrapped the headscarf around his neck,

took a gulp of water and then headed back to their hole in the fence.

He hiked five minutes along the perimeter until he came to the entrance beneath the guard tower. He squinted but couldn't make out if anyone was actually in the tower.

He raised a fist and pounded on the metal. "Open these fuckin gates!" he yelled at the top of his lungs.

He heard scurrying on the other side, several bodies moving quickly past the cutout designs in the heavy metal. At the sides, he saw two guards look through the fencing at him. No one appeared in the guard tower.

He banged on the gate again. "Hey assholes! Open the fuck up!"

"Brother?" came a voice at the side, behind the fence.

Garrett noticed a man in his twenties addressing him.

"I'm not your fuckin' brother. Open this fuckin' gate right now."

"We don't allow strangers—"

"Bull shit! If I was a pretty girl, I'd be in there already. Now get your handler and get someone to open these doors. I got business with your leader."

He didn't have to wait long before the enormous metal doors slowly creaked open.

He recognized Nelson Bales standing before him,

smiling, with his arms outstretched. "Welcome, traveler. What can I do for you this beautiful morning?" The man looked genuinely happy to see him.

With his flowing robes, long locks, and good looks, he reminded Garrett of Moses from that motion picture his grandmother had taken him to see when he was a boy. He'd been watching Bales' face until he saw something moving lower down. Around the pastor's neck and shoulders twisted and wrapped a very large, slow-moving python.

Okay, not Moses, then. You're the fuckin' devil. It was too late to change course. He'd committed. Time to stick to the plan everyone was counting on him for. He prepared, took a deep breath, and shouted to the whole world, wanting to make it loud enough to wake up everyone in the valley.

"I came to get my girlfriend," Garrett boomed. "I'm taking her home. She belongs with me."

Heads turned. People stood frozen in place. Morning smoke from a cooking fire fingered its way through the clearing, reminding him of some death scenes overseas. From the stillness came the pastor's voice.

"And who might that be?" Bales asked.

"We call her Red." His eyes traveled over the surprised faces of the crowd that had gathered. He didn't see Joshua, of course. But he got a glimpse of Georgette poking her head out from the doorway of a long dorm-looking building. Standing near her was the woman who made his heart leap and his soul burn.

Mimi!

His Invisio squawked.

"Hey, Garrett! Hope you can hear this," came the panicked voice of Tanner. "Just got messaged by my contact at DHS. They've just arrested Mike Bintner, charged him with attempted kidnapping and assault on the president's life. They know you're coming."

CHAPTER 16

MIMI WASN'T PREPARED for Garrett's insertion to go this way. She'd just located and spoken with Georgette, who now looked like a deer in the headlights. The added attention Garrett was bringing was going to make it impossible for her speak to the teen. She put her finger to her lips, hoping Georgette would get the warning, and slipped around the side of the building, out of sight of Pastor Bales.

Georgette's relief was now going to be wiped out.

Think! What am I supposed to do?

Garrett told her last night her mic was still working, so she gave Tanner and whomever else was listening what she could, lowering her voice to a whisper. "Contacted Georgette. She's unharmed, willing and able to help. Now she's scared to death. Stays in the long girls' dorm by the entrance to the garden area, and she desperately wants to leave, and she has a friend who wants to go with her," she whispered, searching for anyone who could see or hear her. Then she added, "Garrett just hit the bee hive."

Mimi figured someone might have appreciation for what he'd just done and how she'd have to adjust to the situation.

She ran down the rear of the large dorm building and emerged at the other end, strolling to the clearing and into the line of sight of everyone. While she did so, the heavy metal entrance doors closed behind Garrett with a boom that shook the ground, taking away his escape option.

She reached down deep to find the strength to walk toward Garrett. A lot could happen in that space between where she was and where he stood. She was fully exposed to any ill intent someone in this crazy group might desire. But she vowed it wouldn't impede her forward progress as she continued to walk.

Garrett didn't move, didn't show any emotion, unlike the evening before. His powerful arms scared and tatted and corded by years of focused workouts, hung at his sides. Those arms had held her last night until she could unwind, made her believe again in the magic of the stars and all the things she'd told herself she wanted some day. To have someone so strong move her body so intensely was a gift she'd always cherish.

But none of that mattered now. She was her father's daughter, and all she could do was continue moving forward. A young girl's foolish mistake had put them all in jeopardy. She couldn't change that. But she might be able to change the outcome, if she was smart, brave and lucky. If she trusted that Garrett knew what he was doing.

Mimi hoped Georgette could now see what was being sacrificed for her and what could be lost because of her actions.

Even Bales remained motionless, following her trajectory. His eyes flickered to the side briefly. Mimi didn't pay attention to it, instead focused on Garrett's face. His steady eyes brought her courage.

A few yards to her right, several men rushed at her, grabbing her by the arms and attempting to pull her away. Bales remained still.

But Garrett darted straight for the group of four Mimi struggled with. She kicked behind her and lunged with her knee, aiming for one man's balls. Garrett yanked one man's arm from his shoulder socket as a deafening crack echoed throughout the clearing. Some of the audience who had gathered reacted to the sound.

With one opponent screaming at his feet, Garrett kicked another attacker in the throat, causing him to pitch forward, spewing blood and teeth before his body collapsed, motionless.

A gun appeared, and Garrett kicked it free. He

broke the man's forearm over his knee with another satisfying crunch. The fourth man released Mimi and jumped on Garrett's back, trying to punch the sides of his head. Unfortunately for him he was short. Garrett grabbed his shirt at the shoulders and swung him over his head, landing him hard in the dirt on his back. The man didn't move. Next, Garrett retrieved the attacker's gun and quickly tucked it into the waistband of his jeans.

And then he looked at her. She knew he could only spare a second. "You okay?"

Mimi was shaking but nodded her head. She felt scratches on her upper arm that started to bleed.

Garrett swung around, surveying their audience, his back to her, arms out to the sides, ready and watching for anyone else who might take a run at them.

Of course, there were no takers.

Bales began to clap. "Well done. These were some of my finest." He tried to look entertained, but Mimi saw the bitterness and deep-seated dislike for how his henchmen had been so easily disabled. She took her cue from Garrett and waited for his decision, while the man at their feet groaned in agony. She suspected he was waiting for help to arrive.

Two young men came to the screaming man's aid, carrying him away from the clearing. Bales held out his palms as if to stop anyone else from coming forward and then approached her.

"Well, Red?" The man's eyes were hard, mismatching his brittle smile. "Your boyfriend, or is it exboyfriend, has come to claim you. If I were you, I'd certainly not disappoint him."

Mimi found courage enough to shout, "He's *not* my boyfriend," which got Garrett's shocked attention.

"Not exactly the way to thank someone who has come to defend your honor, is it? But never mind," Bales shouted.

Mimi noticed the python wrapped around Bales' upper body was moving, slowly unwinding and considering a safer location. Garrett was focused on the reptile as well. Bales gave her an evil grin, stroking his pet. Then he scanned the surrounding area, including the treetops at the perimeter.

"We have some business to discuss. Why don't you bring your team in, Commander? No need for the charade any longer."

Mimi's stomach lurched.

How did they know about the team? Just then, Georgette was brought to the clearing with a pistol pointed at her head.

Mimi heard Garrett swear. Her body began to shake again, and her mouth became parched.

"So this is how we settle things here. We might lose

round one, but round two is definitely in our favor."
The pastor added, "So bring them in, Commander or
this little lady will be sacrificed."

Garrett mumbled under his breath then called off
names, "Fuzzy, Luke and Cornell, stand down. Come
on in."

It took several minutes, but Mimi saw all three of
the team members slowly file in, one by one, from
different hiding places within the encampment.

Cornell was the last to arrive. His duty bag was torn
from him as he approached with his hands above his
head. Fuzzy and Luke were also disarmed and pushed
farther into the center.

"I was told there were four," the pastor sneered.

"You have one of my men," said Garrett defiantly.
He chanced a quick glance in Mimi's direction and
gave a slight nod. She caught the signal to be ready for
something unexpected.

"Take the women to the house," Bales barked to his
men.

Mimi felt another grip on her arm as she and
Georgette were forced to leave the circle, heading for
the garden area.

Suddenly, a drone appeared overhead, and dropped
a metal object that flashed and then filled the clearing
with bright orange smoke. The drone changed direction and swooped down, nearly knocking Bales in the

head. Garrett barked an instruction to his team she couldn't make out. The pastor stumbled but regained his footing, adjusting the heavy snake as he did so.

As smoke continued to fill the area, Mimi felt her captor's grip loosen and then saw him hit the ground. People in the crowd started to scream and disperse. Garrett's outstretched hand appeared out of the orange cloud, pulling her arm toward him. She ran beside him as fast as she could as they darted through the chaos and found shelter behind a large gravel truck where the others, including Georgette, waited.

Mimi embraced her young student, who had begun to shake, her teeth chattering.

Cornell had picked up his bag, unzipped it, and distributed a pistol to Fuzzy. Luke and Garrett showed they had retrieved theirs.

Georgette began to lose control and was becoming too difficult to handle. Mimi was afraid she'd bolt away at any moment.

Luke spoke to her calmly. "Just breathe, Georgette, and drink." He gave her water and brushed her face with a wet cloth. Garrett studied her condition carefully.

"We gotta go. Luke, can she make it?" Mimi knew they were losing precious time.

"Yup." He grabbed her shoulders. "Gotta run, sweetheart. Can you help me out?"

Georgette looked confused, and Luke shrugged.

"Tanner, we're clear. There are about fifty innocents, including kids. We can't protect them all. Things are going to shit here. Get that backup rescue team up here ASAP."

Then he turned to Cornell. "You got more smoke?"

Cornell responded by rolling a cannister toward the center. It began spewing dark smoke.

"Nice drone work, Tanner," Garrett whispered into his earpiece then listened to instructions. "Thanks, man. I'm going to pay you back proper when we get the hell out of here. You got a dozen beers coming. See you at the bottom, brother."

He turned to the group, addressing her first. His eyes were all business. "You three," he motioned to Fuzzy, Georgette, and Mimi, "get to the first greenhouse and stay down on your hands and knees. Luke and I are going for Josh. Cornell, get to the long warehouse beyond and light that thing up. Tanner's sending a SWAT and fire crew to nab the bad guys at the main entrance. We grab a truck and get our asses out the back way. He'll meet us back in town."

He made eye contact with each of the men. "Any questions?"

When no one answered, he asked Mimi. "Ladies? You gotta help us out and run like hell. Take care of old Fuzzy here."

Georgette interrupted him, finally becoming more present. "What about my friend, Mallory?"

He winced. "Honey, I'm not sure—"

"But I promised I'd take her with us."

"Give me a gun. I'll go with her," Mimi jumped in. She could see resources were running thin and time was dwindling away.

"Fuckin' no way. Can't take the chance." He swore.

"Hey, boss, we're getting some attention," Cornell whispered.

"Change of plans," barked Garrett. "Fuzzy and Luke get Josh." He addressed Cornell. "Cover us. We'll meet you at the warehouse."

Garrett put his arm around Georgette and nearly carried her along with him. Mimi stayed close behind. They heard exchange of gun fire but kept going. Each loud noise or scream made Georgette jump. Garrett kept a steady arm around her waist, pulling her forward.

They crossed paths with people running like wild horses, bumping into each other and tripping over steps and tools in their way. The place was in total chaos. Mimi heard the drone still buzzing overhead.

They arrived at the entrance to the dorm. Once inside, the building appeared to be abandoned.

"Mallory?" Georgette called out softly.

"Oh. My. God. Get me out of here," said a frail

voice as they watched Mallory scramble from under one of the beds. She was still wearing her nightgown and had bare feet.

"No time for shoes, honey. We gotta go."

He pushed all three of them through the doorway. Mimi was confused where they were, but Mallory helped with Georgette and led them all down the path to the gardens and the greenhouses beyond.

As they rounded a curve, the wall on a cinderblock structure blew up, sending small chunks of concrete raining down on all of them. Mimi saw Fuzzy and Luke drag Joshua through the smoke. It took both of them to carry former undercover agent. His face was swollen. Dark brown stains covered the front of his tee shirt. His feet were bloody.

Garrett directed them to bypass the greenhouses and head for a row of delivery trucks parked at the side of the large warehouse. Cornell ran toward them just as the building exploded behind him. The force of the blast sent him flying, but he was able to get up, limping.

"What the hell was that?" she asked.

"There's going to be a lot of potheads in Oregon mighty disappointed," Cornell coughed, catching his breath.

Garrett jumped into the first truck and got it started while Luke and Fuzzy unlatched the roll-up door in the rear and started helping everyone get inside. Cornell hopped up in the passenger seat as Mimi climbed into the back just before Luke pulled down the metal door. She fell against Georgette and Mallory when the truck spun its wheels and suddenly lurched forward.

Mallory and Georgette huddled together, consoling one another. Luke turned on a headlamp, which gave them some light. He handed out what water he had left and then unzipped his medic kit and began working on Joshua. Mimi scooted over to give him a hand wiping blood and dirt from Joshua's face with a damp cloth while Luke sterilized the wounds, applied pads and strips to some of the deeper cuts and then gave him an injection.

At a distance, the faint sound of sirens was reassuring and growing louder. That meant the women and children they'd had to leave behind would be tended and cared for.

As the truck started to descend off the mountain, Mimi felt her phone ping with a call from Tanner. She'd forgotten that she'd stuck the device in the front pocket of her overalls.

She hit the return button that didn't pick up.

But at least they had phone reception. For now, their team was safe.

CHAPTER 17

G ARRETT ARRANGED FOR the team to use portable showers stored in Klamath Falls for wildfire first responders and to get clean clothes. But he wouldn't allow himself the luxury of a nice, hot shower until he saw that Tanner was back safely with the motorhome. He'd tried to call him but failed to make contact. They were also too far away for the Invisio bandwidth.

He expected Tanner to beat them to the bottom. Ten minutes later, he wondered if the old motorhome had experienced mechanical problems. He checked with the battalion commander on the fire brigade, who stated they hadn't seen the beast.

But when a half hour passed and there was still no communication, Garrett started to worry. He kicked himself all over the block for not running back up there immediately.

Cornell approached from behind. "You hear from him at all?" he asked.

"No, and that's not like Tanner. He's got all that shit up there, all our recordings and the satellite equipment, the printers and a record of everything we did." With his hands on his hips, facing the eastern foothills from where they'd come, Garrett knew he had to go back. "Something's wrong," he whispered.

Fuzzy approached. "You check with the Commander in charge of the cleanup?"

"They didn't know to look for him. Never saw the motor home. I'm worried some of Bales group started down the mountain and caught Tanner before he could leave."

Cornell had an idea. "These guys use drones to check on wildfires all the time. Let me see if I can arrange one."

"Good idea. But I don't want to wait anymore for some kind of BS clearance. Besides, Tanner was our drone guy."

Garrett called Luke over. "Can you arrange an EMT to travel with them?"

"Piece of cake. That mean we're all going up the hill?"

"It does."

"Consider it done." Luke ran into the fire station.

Mimi and the two girls emerged from the women's showers. In spite of his worries, he smiled down on her. "Feel better?"

"Much," she beamed and gave him a hug. "Thanks for getting us out of there. I never doubted you."

Garrett knew she wouldn't like what he had to say next. She reacted when he stiffened at her touch.

"Mimi, Tanner's not back yet."

"Oh my God, Garrett. He tried to call me. I forgot—"

"When?"

"When we left the camp. I was in the back. The phone pinged. I tried to redial him, and didn't reach him. I completely forgot. I'm so sorry."

"Well, we're done waiting. We were supposed to have a quick facetime DHS debriefing before the flight home, but now I've got a man we've left behind, and that's my job to make sure he gets home."

"What does that mean?" she asked.

"Means you return on the plane to D.C. with Joshua and the two girls."

Luke whistled and gave him the thumbs-up.

"We're sending an EMT with you, just in case. You guys will be safe."

"And what about you and the rest of the guys?"

"We're going back to get him. Gotta leave right now."

He saw her brave acknowledgement of what had to be done and her fear for his safety. He'd been enjoying the fantasy of what it would be like to spend a slow afternoon and evening clean and in some fresh sheets, undisturbed. He quickly pushed it out of his mind.

She awkwardly kissed him good-bye, a safe but very chaste kiss. They parted, and she walked away.

"Wait a minute, Mimi," he called after her. They met in the middle. He wrapped his arms around her and planted a huge kiss, which developed into a desperate need to feel her tight against him, all her soft parts filling his hard ones.

Mimi fanned herself when they separated. Her flushed face broke out in a sexy smile. "Better. Much better, Garrett."

"I'll see you soon." He had to turn away and head the opposite direction or he'd do something inappropriate.

GARRETT HAD THE authority to commandeer vehicles and equipment, but the theft of a whole mobile unit full of government surveillance equipment on such a sensitive project wasn't something DHS would look too kindly on, so he placed a call to Silas Branson.

"Great job getting Sorrel back. The president is pleased, Garrett. I knew I could count on you. And you did it with that sonofabitch Mike nearly blowing the whole mission."

"Well, before we start celebrating, we're missing Tanner."

"I thought he was with you."

"He was to meet us down the hill. He was in the mobile unit. We went out the back way. He was on the front side, and he hasn't returned yet."

"Shit."

"I'm going back—everyone is, except Joshua, who got beat up pretty bad. The girls' plane is leaving within the hour."

"Yeah, I just got word. The president wants to be there."

"So just letting you know, I have to fix it, and I will. I promise."

"Don't mess this up, Garrett. The future of this program is riding on your shoulders."

"I think about that every minute, Si. I won't let you down."

All the way back to the encampment, Garrett thought of how many times they'd planned operations, and how many times things had gone wrong, just like this. It wasn't just now and then, it was *every* time. In fact, in his twenty-year career, things *never* went the way it was planned, except once. There was always some ass-chewing from the headshed when they came back from those missions, because most of the people directing their ops had never seen combat. They got the mission done, but sometimes they had to stand there and get yelled at because it didn't happen the way it was supposed to.

But there was that one time, that miracle, when, finally, one mission actually went the way it was supposed to. He knew that day would never happen again. They all knew it.

Having to adjust to ever-changing conditions or poor intel was what he'd learned to be good at. This mission was no different. Except now, if it didn't turn out, he wouldn't be fucking up his career, he'd be fucking up everyone else's on the team. The Bone Frog Command might cease to be. He wasn't going to let that happen. But he also wouldn't let one of his men languish or get lost, no matter what the rest of the outcome was.

He hoped to God it was a false alarm, was just something wrong with the electrical system or the motor on the beast. But in his heart, he knew it was bad news. Tanner hadn't communicated with them because he couldn't.

They'd been given a National Forest Service vehicle with a king cab. Trees at the side of the road were covered in red dust from all the emergency vehicles traveling up and down. Twice he stopped personnel to inquire on their teammate.

No one had seen the vehicle, or Tanner.

Garrett decided against alerting too many other departments. The fewer people who knew what they'd done, the better. He continued up the bumpy road, slowing down and then stopping in a small shoulder so they could travel the rest of the way on foot.

Everyone piled out and climbed a few yards. Just before they arrived at the clearing, he heard the motor on the coach start up. Through the trees, he could see it moving toward them at a high rate of speed and knew it wasn't Tanner at the wheel.

"Take the shot, Cornell."

His sharpshooter carefully pulled out his sniper rifle and, with total calm, drilled the driver in the forehead. The motor coach careened on its side and nearly rolled completely over. They could hear breaking glass and equipment being thrown all over the place inside. Shards of glass exploded over the road as the coach rested upside down.

Cornell stood guard while Fuzzy and Garrett ripped a door off its hinges. Smoke began to float up to the sky, and he could smell leaking fuel.

Garrett's heart sank as nothing moved inside. Luke jumped in behind him and checked for signs of life. The driver was dead. Two other men were unconscious but still had a pulse. Garrett overturned the table and tossed the printer to the side, trying to find Tanner in the debris. Blood spatters were everywhere, but there was no sign of Tanner.

Fuzzy nodded to the closed bedroom door. Garrett

gulped down the smokey air and kicked it open.

The mattress was covering a huge mound beneath it. Garrett knew there was a body there. Pure adrenaline flowed in his veins when he tossed the heavy mattress one-handed, afraid for what he'd find, but knowing he had to do it.

The body beneath the mattress was not that of Tanner, but Pastor Bales. His face was grotesquely purple, his lips blue and his eyes bloodshot, which surprised Garrett at first.

"Holy hell!" shouted Fuzzy.

Garrett heard Cornell shout out, wanting to know what they'd found.

From under the debris, Pastor Bales' python emerged, it's bloodied and cut body leaving a red trail as it found a hole big enough in the frame and silently exited.

"I hate snakes," whispered Garrett.

"So where's Tanner?" asked Luke.

Garrett scrambled to get out, careful not to get snagged on the twisted metal and glass everywhere. "Come on. Let's get back up to our site."

The forestry vehicle's off-road tires grabbed the dirt just enough to keep them going forward without careening off the edge of the drive. At the clearing where they'd parked, they found Tanner's battered body, lying in a pool of his own blood. Luke ran to the man's side. Garrett stayed in the truck, his forehead pressed against the steering wheel, praying they weren't too late.

"He's still alive!" shouted Luke.

CHAPTER 18

MIMI WANTED TO see her classroom first thing the next day. It was a Saturday and school wasn't in session. The halls were vacant even though the bells still rang.

She walked down the aisles, touching the desks of her students, even feeling the chalkboard's dusty residue between her fingers. Papers to correct waited in her inbox. Someone had been feeding the turtle one of her students gave her last year. She smelled the books and heard the sounds outside of a landscaper mowing the Academy's lawn. So much had happened, she longed for something normal. A reminder of what her life used to be.

What is normal?

All her concerns about teaching and her complaints about her single lifestyle faded away. Nothing was as she'd left it. And that was because she was forever changed.

Now she understood what her father had done all those years on the Teams. She understood what kind of man it took to be able to do this sort of thing over and over again and then come home to a wife and kids. Nothing was ever normal for those guys. Risking their lives every time was just part of the job.

It wasn't hers. That she knew for sure. She also understood the toll it had taken on her mother to care for such an intense man. Could she do it, she wondered? Mimi wasn't sure.

Her cell rang.

"Mimi? This is President Collier."

"Good morning, Mr. President."

"Liz and I just wanted to thank you for all you've done to help us get Georgette back. I don't quite have the proper words but let me say this. If you need anything at all, anything, you understand, something for your classroom or for yourself, you know where to call, okay?"

"Thank you. That's very nice." She knew the president was busy, so she began to sign off. "Well I hope she gets lots of rest. It was a very harrowing time for her."

"She wants to come right back to your classroom," he said. "That's a great testament to you, Mimi."

"I think she should take some time off and process everything. Sorry, but that's my advice, for what it's worth." She suddenly was embarrassed at having given the president advice on raising his daughter. He didn't have the option of taking his family on some relaxing vacation. He had the whole country to run. Who was she to even have an opinion? "I'm sorry, sir. That wasn't very well said."

"No, I completely agree, but her mother disagrees. We're discussing our options. What about you? Are you going to jump right back into your teaching?"

That's when it hit her. What *was* she going to do?

ON HER WAY back to her apartment, she resisted the temptation to call Garrett. He hadn't called her last night when they arrived in D.C. Someone from DHS called to let her know everyone got home safely and she thanked them. He'd asked them to do that. But he couldn't do it himself.

She'd taken a hot bath and fell asleep reading one of her romance books. She woke up realizing she'd ruined another Kindle as she eyed it lying at the bottom of the tub.

She watched a little news, just to be sure no mention of the president's daughter's disappearance was leaked anywhere. Mimi called her friend, Carmen, and they made a date for dinner and a movie. Halfway through, she couldn't remember the storyline and then fell asleep in her chair.

Over pizza and a beer, Carmen started to probe. "They were very cryptic about your absence, Mimi. Is something going on?"

She almost burst out laughing. It was so absurd. "Nothing's going on, I swear it. Everything's just fine."

When she got home, she fell on her bed, rolled over, kicked off her shoes, and stared at the ceiling.

Mimi knew it was stress, but it didn't make it any easier to feel anything at all. She knew that in time, she'd unthaw.

As she lay there, a tear started forming in her left eye, and she focused on it. Then her other eye teared up, and her chest began to hurt. But it wasn't her chest. It was her heart.

She was missing that one thing that would bring her back to life quicker. She missed that connection. She'd had a sip from the well of belonging, turning her inside out and opening her up to what could be. And now she felt the pain of losing it.

Then she saw her father's face. She saw the two of them, best friends, on the beach laughing and wrestling, kicking sand and pulling each other into the surf. She missed all of it.

Her eyes erupted, her lip quivered, and her chest heaved, her lungs trying to fill with air between her sobs.

She knew it would be like this going forward if

Garrett had decided he was done with her. There wouldn't be any point in chasing him. And she'd hate herself afterwards if she did. It was going to have to be his move, and she'd just deal with it, if that move never came.

Life isn't fair, like she'd told her students.

She knew what to expect. She'd have these lonely evenings, and then things would calm down before erupting again for no good reason at all. That's how it was going to be. Until everything got processed. The ups and the downs would blend into one, and she could function or lie to herself she was functioning normally.

And, although it hurt to have hope, she was glad she did. Garrett had introduced her to that magic, the intensity of a life of action and honor. A life well-lived. She was not going to settle for anything or anyone else, even if she had to wait forever.

Because he was worth it.

CHAPTER 19

G ARRETT'S REPORT WAS thirty pages long. He sat for several three-hour meetings while the Secret Service and DHS pieced together how Mike Bitner had gotten so close to the president. Every communication he'd had with the man was examined and analyzed.

Bales had used his son's exposure as a summer intern in Mike's office to extract payback for what he'd suffered when their Texas compound was raided and shut down. Mike did it for the money, but Bales was the truly more dangerous man. He did it for revenge, Garrett was told.

Poor Loren—Bales' son—was the pawn in the game, the one who was able to worm his way into Georgette's inner circle just by sneaking in an unde- tected cell phone so they could text message each other. The plan was so simple they'd all missed it. The boy had been obsessed with her ever since that summer when they met. He suffered from delusions like his father, the pastor, that one day Bales would allow him to marry her. He had no idea that Bales had planned her murder, not their wedding.

In the meantime, Bales intended to destroy that symbol of power that had shut him down: the White House. It didn't matter who the First Family was, he would never stop getting even.

Thank God he was dead, thought Garrett.

Like all missions accomplished, not everything about it was successful. Two members of the team had been seriously injured, and there was the loss of a great deal of very expensive equipment.

But Georgette Collier had been safely returned, and the general public never knew what kind of danger she'd been in. The incident allowed staffers to implement changes in protocol that would ensure the safety of this and future president's households going forward.

He was asked all the tough questions about the Bone Frog Command. Did he consider it a success? Was there a place for this type of operation going forward?

"Yes," Garrett answered the secretary of Homeland Security. "This mission would have failed if we had too many people involved in it. If we hadn't had individuals who were expert in their specialized fields, with the background, experience and training to work together," he said.

"What would you have done differently?" he was asked.

"First, I'll tell you what I wish we had. And it's something we'll never ever get, no matter how many times we try."

"What's that?"

"Accurate intel. We didn't have it overseas. We'd get into these places and everything we were told about the mission was inaccurate or based on assumptions that were false. Here, I was working with and depending on someone who turned out to be the whole reason we were called in in the first place, sir."

"And how do you avoid that, Tierney?"

"You know how you stop the Federal Reserve from being robbed?" He was going to use Tanner's story as an example.

"Enlighten me, Tierney."

"You can't stop them, sir. You just make it impossible for them to get out in less than a half-hour and hope like hell that gives you enough time to catch them."

"So with respect to these missions, how do you improve the quality of the intel?"

"You don't. You hire guys who can get 'er done anyway. Who are used to getting blown and adjusting, never giving up. To properly react to some threats to the homeland, we don't have time to go through approvals and levels of bureaucracy. That's why you need a stealth force to cut through all the BS and not cry about it. We were trained to do the impossible, and that's what we do."

"Oversight?"

"That's a dirty word, sir. Oversight is a term for not knowing what the hell you were doing in the first place."

"Would you consider working on this team going forward?" the secretary asked him.

"Possibly, but each time, you have to get a team put together for each scenario. You can't have the same people every time, because it requires different skills, depending on the job."

"So, what's next for you? Are you willing to be on call?"

"I'm going back to Sonoma County, sir, and I'm going to plant the vegetables I didn't get in before I came out here. I'm going to drink some beer, fix my well, probably get a couple new hens. And if the telephone never rings again asking me to do one of these, I'll die a happy man, sir."

"How about your personal life? I understand there was a budding romance."

Garrett smirked at the question. He'd guessed some of Tanner's recordings had surfaced from the wreck and he could see now he was right. He wasn't exactly proud of it, but that was okay.

"Sir, there was, and is, a romance—not just budding, but in full raging bloom. But if I spend all my time going to interviews and writing reports, she's going to die an old maid, or some other Bone Frog will nab her before I get the chance to convince her I'm the one."

He saw the secretary had his eyebrows raised.

"You do know, it's the woman who chooses?"

The secretary sat back, threw his head back, and laughed.

Garrett stood. "It's been nice chatting with you, and I'm available if you need more information. Beyond that, sir, it's none of your damned business."

CHAPTER 20

M IMI'S CELL RANG but she'd gotten so many solicitation calls for credit card deals and free energy audits she stopped answering them and let them all go to voicemail. Besides, her gloved hands were dirty. She was planting some broccoli in little pots on her patio. She'd ordered several gardening books online as well.

It had been four days since they returned from Oregon. She had prepared for classes after taking the following week off. She stopped expecting a call from Garrett.

When she came inside, tossing her gloves in the sink, she checked the phone and was shocked to see Garrett's number on the screen.

Her hands started to shake. She hit redial.

His warm, chesty voice made her spine tingle. "Well, hello there. Did I catch you at a bad time?"

She brushed hair off her face and felt particles of soil fall down her front. "I—I was just outside. I've decided to try my hand at a little gardening."

"Really?"

Was he playing with her?

"What are you planting?"

"Broccoli. I thought that would be a no-brainer to try. That's what the nursery said, anyway."

"You can't grow broccoli in D.C. in the fall. It's too late."

Something defensive reared up inside.

"Mimi? You still there?"

"So what should I have planted?"

"It's not *what* you chose to plant but *where* you chose to plant it, my dear."

She thought about that for a bit. Was he saying—?

"If you come out here to California, I'll show you how to plant decent broccoli. I can show you a lot of other things to plant too."

Her heart fluttered. She took in a deep breath and tried to let it out without him hearing how anxious she was. "I sense you have some ulterior motive behind all this."

"I do. I most definitely do. And here I thought I was being so cagy about everything."

"Well, I start school after next week. How long a visit are we talking about here?"

He sighed and slowly whispered, "I was thinking forty, maybe fifty years."

CHAPTER 21

"BROCCOLI? YOU BOUGHT more broccoli? You've already got a bunch of it," said Geronimo.

"Humor me. Just put them out there. I'll plant them tomorrow."

"Okay Commander, but has this turned into some kind of superfood now? You never plant so much before."

"I've acquired a taste for it all of a sudden." Garrett handed off the two six packs of the vegetable plus two others and brushed his hands together. "I'm going to finish unloading. Then I have to get inside to make dinner."

"You want I should clean the patio? I can hose it off—"

"No, you did a great job today. Everything looks great. As a matter of fact, take a few days off, Geronimo. I'm going to be staying home awhile. I'll call you when I get back to fixing things."

"Okay." Geronimo shrugged. "I think something must be bery bery wrong. First, you bring home all that broccoli, and now flowers to plant."

"Not flowers. Snapdragons."

"But the summer is over, Commander. You don't plant snapdragons in the fall."

"You do if you want nice blooms in the spring. Just like you plant daffodils in the fall for spring bloom."

"Yes, but you don't like flowers. You told me that one time before."

"I know what I'm doing. I think." Garrett brought in the rest of his groceries, sneaking a bouquet of roses under his arm.

"Commander!"

Garrett stopped in his tracks. His handyman was pointing at the roses like he was holding a dead animal.

He'd gotten caught fair and square. "So I wasn't entirely truthful with you. I'm having someone over for dinner."

Snooker had been following Garrett around the house and yard, not leaving more than two feet between them ever since he got back. The dog sat and looked up at his master.

Geronimo laughed. "Oh, that dog gonna be jealous. I think he maybe get a broken heart."

Garrett patted the top of his head and managed to open his front door without spilling the grocery bags or dropping the roses. Snooker followed him inside.

He set the roses in a beer pitcher then placed them in the middle of the dining table. He'd laid out the dishes in the morning when he awoke, including the wine glasses he had to wash three times to get all the streaks out. He was using cloth napkins his mother left him.

After putting away the ice cream, half and half and chocolate fudge topping, he began rinsing and then drying the lettuce for the green salad. Geronimo tapped on the kitchen door and it made him jump.

"Okay, I see you in a few days. You want me to do anything else?"

Garrett detected his helper was stalling so he could get a good look at his company. "It will be dark in an hour. How about you get those chickens in the coop a little early, so I don't have to do it later?"

"Sure, sure." Geronimo left.

Garrett turned on the gas barbeque then opened a bottle of red wine to give it time to breathe. He ran upstairs and combed his hair again, pulling down the darker portions over his silver temples, then trimmed his beard when he found two wayward hairs. He brushed his teeth for the third time and then applied aftershave. He sniffed at his armpits and decided they weren't acceptable so applied deodorant and changed his shirt.

"Look at you, you old fart." He was sensitive about the lines around his eyes, but today, he saw lines everywhere. She'd only seen him shirtless one time, and that was before they were intimate. But it had been dark that night in Virginia. And in Oregon, Mimi's little cabin was pitch black. So if everything went as planned, she'd be seeing him tonight for the first time fully naked. Would she find him still attractive, or would she be turned off because he was too old?

He studied his bedroom, glancing over his king-sized bed with his grandmother's quilt he'd brought out of storage and had washed. Garrett thought she'd like that touch. No woman had ever slept in that bed before. Snooker decided it was a good idea to jump up and lay down on the colorful quilt.

"Snooks! Get off the bed."

The dog gave him the sad look.

"Come on, *off!*"

The dog with balls the size of his fist took his time, groaned and looked up at him one more time as if to make sure he wasn't going to change his mind, and then jumped off, sitting by Garrett's side. Garrett smoothed over the divots Snooker had made and re-plumped the pillows.

Geronimo's sister had cleaned the house this morning, something he decided he'd start doing on a weekly basis. She'd also cleaned the windows on the inside while her brother did the outside.

He didn't have much—everything of importance and value to him could be locked in his gun safe downstairs in the study. He hoped she liked the uncluttered look. It was almost spartan.

Garrett skipped downstairs again, Snooker's toes tapping on the wood floors behind him. He turned on the big screen to a country station but kept the volume half what he'd normally listen to alone. Thinking he might have missed something, he scanned the great room, straightening up pillows his mother and grandmother had made. Snooker had started gratefully lounging on them today.

The smoke from the barbeque had created a large white cloud in the backyard, so he turned it down, brushing the grates clean from his last meal. The meat was marinating on the countertop, pushed back far enough so Snooker couldn't help himself to it. That's when he remembered he hadn't given him his supper.

"Come on, Snooks. Let's get you fed."

The happy dog wagged what tail he had left and followed him into the pantry, then back to the kitchen where Garrett mixed the wet and dry food with the powdered hip and joint mix and set the stainless steel bowl for him in the corner. He replenished his water dish beside and waited the whole three minutes while the dog finished the meal.

Hearing a noise outside, he saw the driver he'd hired get out, open the rear door for her, and stand to the side while Mimi stepped out onto his land. She did a 360 degree sweep of the area, a delightful smile gracing her full red lips. Her mahogany hair, still streaked with red coloring, flowed in every direction in the gentle Fall wind. Her red dress draped around her ample curves, scooping just enough in front to show off her graceful neck and enormous chest. The vision before him took his breath away.

Before he could think, he was outside on the porch overhang to greet her and realized too late that he was still barefoot.

Mimi dropped her bag and ran to him. She wrapped her arms around him tight then moved her mouth up to his hungrily and did several touch landings before they locked together in a deep, hot kiss.

The driver behind her cleared his throat. One large suitcase stood by his side.

"Thank you," Garrett said as he dug a twenty out of his back pocket. "That enough?"

"It will be on your credit card. You can do the whole thing on your card, if you like."

"You keep this. Thanks again."

Mimi raised the handle and began wheeling her suitcase toward the front door before Garrett caught up to her and snatched it away. He also grabbed her carryon case.

"Welcome to my place. It's very simple, nothing fancy, but I built this house with my own hands and it suits me. I hope you like it."

She surveyed the gardens, walking from his front door to the right. "It's lovely up here. And look at your garden!"

He let her wander, watched her walk over to the fence and lean into his vegetable plot. The corn was nearly done and had begun to dry out, and the tomatoes still had some red and orange fruits, but the vines were turning brown. He was proud of his lush rows of Chinese cabbage, celery, swiss chard, and broccoli.

She pointed, "Broccoli?"

"Yes ma'am" he said, leaving the luggage and joining her. "And I have more we can plant tomorrow, if you want."

"That's right. You did promise to show me. I'm looking forward to my lesson."

His arms fit so well around her as she leaned back into him, her head resting just under his chin. They viewed the garden together for several quiet seconds.

"I've got lots to show you, Mimi. I don't know where to start," he whispered to the top of her head.

She turned in his arms. "Let's take it slow so I don't miss a thing," she said, her warm brown eyes sparkling in the orange glow of a raging sunset.

He couldn't believe she was here. He'd thought about it, fantasized about it, wondered and stressed about it, and now it was really happening.

"Any speed you want, I'm game, Mimi."

They returned to his porch. He grabbed the luggage and opened the door, but waited for her to step inside first.

He held his breath as she made it to the middle of the great room, stopped, and examined the hand-hewn wooden beams and upper-story windows. She let her fingers slide over the top of his leather couch.

Snookers barked at her as if she hadn't afforded him the respect he was due.

"Oh my. What kind of a dog is that?" she asked as she squatted and held her hand out. Snookers made a beeline for her affection, wagging his stub of a tail so voraciously he couldn't keep his back legs on the ground. She squeezed his ears with her palms.

"He's a Doberpit. Very unique breed," he laughed.

Snookers barked again so Garrett joined the two of them.

"He's beautiful! So affectionate, too." The admiration she was laying on Snooks was not lost on the dog. He scooted closer to her and then leaned against her knees to beg for more. He nearly sent Mimi back on her rear.

"I'd say you made a hit. That's important in this

house," Garrett said.

She stood. "Garrett, this is just beautiful. I can see why you love it here."

"You haven't seen half of it. Tomorrow, we can take the ATV, and I'll show you the rest of the property. I even have a frog pond!"

"Amazing."

"Are you hungry?" he said as he moved to the kitchen. He poured them both a glass of wine.

"Starved," she said as they touched glasses. "Appetite has never been a problem for me, as you can probably tell." She blushed, her eyes facing downward.

"You're perfect, Mimi. You're healthy, glowing, I love your body. I've been thinking about nothing else these past few days."

She sipped her wine. "Tell me more." She wiggled her eyebrows.

"I told you I'd keep my promise—" He stepped closer to her, their thighs brushing against each other. "I said I'd put my fingers and hands, my kisses too, all over every square inch of your body. I intend to do that."

She looked at him over the rim of her glass as she took another sip.

"Really? And then what are you going to do tomorrow?"

HE'D MADE TOO much of a fuss over dinner because they barely took a few bites before it was obvious they both had one thing on their minds. He held her hand as he led her up the stairs to his bedroom.

She gasped as she saw the quilt. "This is lovely, Garrett. Is it family?"

Snooker jumped up into the middle of the bed and lay down.

"Off, Snooker!" Garrett waited for him to exit the room and then he closed the door.

"It belonged to my grandmother. It's really the only thing I have of hers. My mother said she made it."

"I love quilting. I probably never told you."

He slowly walked to her, feeling the heat of her body and smelling the soft perfume of her arousal. "We really haven't done much talking at all. But I think I knew that, somehow, Mimi." He was overwhelmed with the natural beauty of her soft round face. "No one's ever been here before, Mimi. You're the first."

She stood on tiptoes and kissed him tenderly, whispering between their lips, "I didn't realize you were a virgin, Garrett."

He chuckled. He brought his fingers to her cheek then down to her chin and tipped her head back slightly and kissed her. "I've never considered sharing my life with anyone before I met you. I don't even know how well I'll do it. I'm more or less a civilian now—"

"You're never a civilian. You'll always be ready to save someone," she whispered back, her eyes focusing on his lips before they touched again.

"I'm old-fashioned about some things and very closed off to other things I don't want you to have anything to do with. But I've gotten to see the worst of humanity while serving with the best. The two come together. Can't have one without the other. I'm a confusing package, and I admit I'm not very easy-going."

"I'm stubborn too," she said as she placed his palm on her right breast. "I know what I want and I go after it. I don't change my mind, either. I make friends for life, but I can live well alone."

His fingers had slipped into her bra, rubbing the soft surface of her flesh. "Thinking of you all alone makes me ache," he whispered then bent down and kissed her cleavage, beginning to explore with his tongue. "You were made for me, Mimi. I don't ever want you to be alone again. I want to convince you that you belong here, with me."

She inhaled and leaned into him, placing her arms up over his shoulders so he could feel her nippled knotting and waiting for his touch. "I'm going to pretend I've not already made up my mind because I want you to keep convincing me." She kissed him again and then watched his face, giving him the space to say what he'd planned on saying, practiced saying for the past three days.

"Marry me, Mimi. I promise, I'll keep convincing you to say yes for the rest of your life."

Here's an excerpt from Sharon's latest book, SEALed Forever, Book 3 in the Bone Frog Brotherhood, which releases 4-16-19. It's available to order here.

sharonhamiltonauthor.com/sealed-forever

Here's the first chapter for your reading pleasure!

Chapter 1 excerpt, SEALed Forever, Book 3 of the Bone Frog Brotherhood Series:

NAVY SEAL TUCKER Hudson squinted across the beach bonfire that roared taller than any of the men on his SEAL Team 3. He was back—at least in all the ways he could be. He was now forty years of age—a retread. He'd survived the landmines of past deployments, the vacancy of those years off the teams, as well as the grueling BUD/S training re-qualifying for his spot. He was ready for his first mission as a new *silver* SEAL, as the ladies called him. He was a Bone Frog, one of the old guys on SEAL Team 3.

He was ready for the do-over. Told himself he deserved it. But just to add a little gasoline to the fire in his soul, his childhood best friend, Brawley Hanks, was failing. And that's what ate at him.

Brawley had just spent six months in rehab while Tucker completed his SQT, SEAL Qualification Training. His Chief, Kyle Lansdowne, had misgivings about allowing Brawley to go on the next mission to Africa, but since Tucker would be there, he'd overruled a suggestion from higher up to sit him out. This didn't help Tucker's nerves any. He knew it was his job to cover all that up and make those jitters disappear.

He watched the ladies dancing around the bonfire and looked for his wife of two months. Brandy cooed over Dorie and Brawley's little pink daughter while Dorie showed her off. The toddler was fast asleep. Several of the Team's kids jumped to get a look at the child until Dorie knelt and let them stand in a circle and check her out.

Their particular SEAL platoon tradition made them gather at the beach before a new deployment. All the wives, the kids, the close girlfriends and occasionally parents were there. But only those on the inside, in the know. Some had lost loved ones. Some had been injured. Some had suffered too much. But these were the people who held them all together—who would hold Brandy together while he was gone.

The past two years with Brandy had been the hardest but most rewarding years of his life. When he was a younger SEAL, sometimes the ladies made him nervous since he didn't have anyone to come home to. But now that he did, now that he could actually lose something dear to him, it made this little celebration all the more special. He'd missed those evenings under the stars in Coronado, surrounded by life and the promise of living forever.

No one would understand this kind of SEAL brotherhood, Tucker thought. You had to live it to know how it felt to be part of this family. You had to cry and celebrate with these people, tell them things would turn out, somehow. The miraculous would happen, because it always did. That's who they were. There wasn't any other group in the whole world he'd rather be a part of, and he'd tried doing without before. He knew better.

Tucker studied the beautiful, round face of his new bride, and all her other curves that enticingly called to him by firelight. It seemed she grew more and more stunning every day. Her eyes met his, and he glanced down quickly, embarrassed that he might look like a teenage boy. But that's the way he felt. He was back to being the big quiet kid the Homecoming Queen or head cheerleader came over to tease. It used to happen a lot in high school and he'd never gotten used to it.

Chief Petty Officer Kyle Lansdowne took up a seat next to him. His Chief was the most respected man on the team, even more than some of the officers, who were never invited to these events. Kyle had worked hard to make sure Tucker came to his squad. Although slightly younger than Tucker or Brawley, Kyle's experience leading successful campaigns through sticky assignments made him one of Team 3's most valuable assets.

"You nervous?" his LPO asked.

"You asked me that the day of my wedding, remember?"

Kyle nodded.

"I was nervous then." Tucker took a pull on his long-necked beer. "I know what I'm getting into this time." He smiled, which was reflected back to him.

"Well, you know what they say about leading men. Don't ask a question you don't know the answer to first." Kyle clinked his bottle against Tucker's.

They both watched the children fawning over Brawley's daughter, still sleeping by the firelight, tucked in Dorie's arms. Kyle's two were right in the middle of them. Brandy gave Tucker a sexy wave.

"You got a good one, Tucker. I'm really happy for you," Kyle whispered, continuing to follow the ladies.

"You bet I did." Tucker meant every word he uttered. He'd always liked women he could grab onto and squeeze without breaking half her ribs. Brandy had the heart he did and that fierce joy of living, which also matched his own. And she'd earned that because of how she'd fought for every ounce of respect she so richly deserved. She spoke her mind. She loved with abandon, and he was damned lucky to have her in his corner. He was also grateful she let him go off and be a warrior again, just when most friends his age had wives ragged on them to quit.

And that was okay too. The SEAL teams were a revolving door of fresh and old faces, and internal dramas played out every day all over the world. It was sometimes hardest on the families. Men had to consider all of that when they played Varsity.

Kyle searched the crowd.

"I haven't seen him in about twenty minutes," Tucker mumbled. It worried him, too, that Brawley wasn't nearby. "I think he might have gone to get more beer, but that's just a rumor."

He knew Kyle suspected he was making up a safe story, which is why he didn't say a word. Then his Chief slowly turned, facing him. "You let me know if he gets shaky, and I thoroughly suspect he will." Kyle's voice was low, avoiding anyone else's ears.

The two men stared at each other for a few long seconds.

"I got it, Kyle. He's not on his own."

"And you only risk a little. Don't let that go over the edge."

"We don't leave men behind." Tucker knew Kyle

understood what he meant.

"No, we don't. I want you both upright. Both of you, Tucker."

"Roger that."

They gripped hands. Then Kyle broke it off and punched him in the arm.

"Dayam, Tucker. You can stop drinking those protein shakes anytime now."

Tucker liked that thought but dished some trash talk back. "Lannie, it ain't protein shakes. It's her," he said, aiming his beer bottle at Brandy. "You should see how she works me out."

Kyle stood up and then murmured, "I can't unsee that, dammit," and disappeared into the crowd.

Tucker hoped Brawley would show himself soon. His "ghosting" wasn't a good sign. He should be at Dorie's side. Tucker kept searching and then finally spotted Brawley pissing into the surf, which meant he was drunker than he should be.

Come on, Brawley. You're gonna get us both killed.

Brandy was still occupied with the women, and Kyle was having a little nuzzle time with Christy while carrying one of his two on his shoulders. Tucker scrambled to his feet and strolled toward his best friend, who was now throwing rocks into the ocean. His jeans were wet, and he was barefoot.

Brawley Hanks grew up alongside Tucker's family

in Oregon. He couldn't ever remember a time when they weren't best friends. Always competitors when it came to sports and girls, even enlisting in the Navy the same day, they attended the same BUD/S class. They'd planned on getting out after their ten years, but close to the end, Brawley met Dorie, and, well, the poor guy couldn't help himself and got hitched up. She had pushed for the re-signing bonus so they could buy a nice house in Coronado. A beautiful, classy girl with all the wildness Brawley had, Dorie was missing his self-destructive bend.

Tucker wondered at first if their marriage would survive, but as Brawley showed all the signs of getting seriously embroiled in a lusty kind of full-tilt love that made him go stupid and do dumb things like buy flowers, he became convinced his friend had finally been tamed and had given up his wandering ways.

Except that after his last two deployments, Brawley was back to being the bad boy he'd always been before he met Dorie. He drank and chased too much. And although they had high hopes for his rehab, he wasn't as convinced as Brandy or Dorie that his bad days were behind him.

"Hit any fish yet?" he asked Brawley.

"Fuck no," Hanks replied, slurring his words and letting go of another smooth, flat stone. It didn't skip like he'd been aiming to do.

"You know the more you hit the ocean, that ocean is gonna get you back, Brawley."

"I'm registering my complaint."

Tucker had to proceed with caution. He was at one of those turning points. But if Brawley lost it, at least he'd lose it here and save Kyle the trouble of having him sent home in shame. It sucked to be thinking this way just a day from deployment, but it was what it was. No sense sugar-coating it.

"I think your registration is going to the wrong department. Got your branches of service mixed up, Brawley. You should take it up with the man upstairs. Have you had that conversation recently?"

Brawley squinted back at him, as if the moonlight hurt his eyes. He did look like a big teenager, albeit a lethal one.

"I wear the Trident. Poseidon and Davy Jones are my buds. The man upstairs has given up on me."

His challenge hit Tucker in his stomach. *You dumb fuck. Where are you goin?*

He walked to within inches of Brawley's hulking form. Inhaling deeply, he worked to calm himself down so it would be effective. He knew he only could say this once, so he made sure Brawley didn't misunderstand his steely stare.

"I'm going to remind you that you just brought a daughter into the world. What kind of a world do you want her to grow up in, you old fart? You want her to grow up with an angry son-of-a-bitch for a father, like you did, Brawley?"

His best friend started to interrupt him, and Tucker grabbed his ears and spit out his message.

"Or were you thinkin' you'd check out over there in that shit African red clay, making Dorie a widow and your daughter fatherless? Maybe causing the death of one or more of your friends who have pledged their lives to save your dumb ass. You willing to take us all with you? You want to be that kind of best friend to me, Brawley? Or, are you gonna man-up?"

Tucker released Brawley's ears and pivoted like a Color Guard. He thanked his lucky stars he hadn't gotten clobbered with that delivery and called it good. Whatever Brawley did next was up to him.

It was just something that had to be delivered *before* they left for Africa. After they were there, it would be too late.

Tucker had done all he could.

If you enjoyed that excerpt, you can order your book here.

sharonhamiltonauthor.com/sealed-forever

But Wait!! There's more. Did you know Sharon bundles all her series books so you can enjoy binge reading? And, all these bundled books have audio books (which you can get at a discount if you have the digital copy by some retailers). If you already know you want to read more about the Brotherhood, Sharon's original SEAL series, here's how you can get bundled up!

Ultimate SEAL Collection #1 (Books 1-4 with 2 novellas) Order here.
sharonhamiltonauthor.com/Ultimate1

Ultimate SEAL Collection #2 (3 novels) Order here.
sharonhamiltonauthor.com/Ultimate2

Or, for those of you who just want to read one book at a time, in order, here's the next one. And don't forget to leave a review!

Did you enjoy SEAL Love's Legacy? Be sure to follow along the rest of the books in this Silver SEALs Series, starting with Maryann Jordan's SEAL Together. Here's an excerpt from the first chapter.

CHAPTER 1

THE SUN HAD set over Caspian Lake in Vermont, and Eric Lopez looked up from his book, noticing that the evening shadows had also deepened. Sliding off his reading glasses, no longer able to see the book in his hand, he placed both items on the arm of the Adirondack chair. Sitting on his deck, facing the water, he propped his feet up on the rail and watched as the moon began to rise.

Leaning over, he picked up the glass tumbler he had sat next to him and gave it a slight swirl to mix the water with the Scotch whiskey. Taking a sip, he continued to watch as the moon cast its reflection over the water. He appreciated the view, the quiet of the evening, and the whiskey.

The view was one of the main reasons he had bought the cabin several years ago. It had been strange, having traveled the world for over twenty years in the US Navy—most of those as a SEAL—to begin again, as a civilian, needing to find a place to live. His parents had passed away years before, and his only sibling, his sister, lived near Washington DC. While he did not mind paying her visits, he had no desire to live in an overcrowded, overpriced metropolis.

When trying to decide where he should purchase a home, he took a map of the United States, closed his eyes, and slapped his finger down on the paper. When he opened his eyes, he saw that his forefinger was pointing at Vermont. With a shrug, he had figured it was as good as any place to settle.

He lucked out when he had found the two-bedroom cabin nestled in five acres of wooded land. The back of his house faced Caspian Lake, and the front was far enough away from the road that it could not be seen. The realtor had extolled the virtues of the upgraded kitchen and bathrooms, as well as the tall stone fireplace in the living room.

Instead, he had walked to the windows near the back, looked out over trees and had appreciated that he could clearly see the lake just behind the property. *I didn't give a shit about the kitchen or bathrooms, but the view…hell, yeah.* Turning around, he had immediately shut her up with the words, "I'll take it."

The quiet atmosphere was another bonus. He could not hear any traffic on the road, nor any neighbors around. Occasionally, on a busy summer day, jet skis and boats carrying noisy vacationers would encroach on his reverie, but where he lived was away from the major vacation spots. The call of birds, the scampering of woodland animals through the leaves, and deer moving through the brush were the only sounds he wanted to hear and, most of the time, that was what he got.

And, of course, the Scotch whiskey. Not a heavy drinker, he had nonetheless acquired the taste for the fine scotch during his SEAL days. At the end of a mission, his team would gather together, pull out whatever glasses they could get their hands on, and pour a splash for each of them. Toasting their success, they sipped the whiskey, enjoying the smokiness and burn. They might go raise hell later but, for a few moments together, they shared a drink.

Sipping the last dregs from his glass, he placed his hands on the arms of his chair and hoisted his body upward. His knee twinged like it always did, but he ignored it as he snagged his tumbler, book, and reading glasses on his way inside. Closing the sliding glass door, he flipped the security bar into place. Setting his alarm by the panel near the door, he moved into the kitchen.

The upgraded kitchen might not have sold him on the home but, after he moved in, he appreciated the work the previous owners had accomplished. Oak cabinets, granite countertops, along with a new stove, dishwasher, and refrigerator. He did not have a gourmet palate, nor did cooking provide great pleasure, but he did like to eat and eat well.

He double checked the windows and front door, security habits long since ingrained still in place. Moving through the bedroom, he continued into the bathroom. Another room that had enjoyed the upgrades from the previous owners, it had been expanded to include a large tiled shower, soaking tub, private toilet, and a double sink. It was a strange habit, but he kept his toiletries to one side of the counter, almost as though a partner would want to use the other sink. But there was no partner, just him.

After a quick shower, he stood at the sink and stared into the mirror. Not the type of man to normally spend much time looking at himself, he felt compelled in that moment to see if he was still the man he used to be.

His body was still muscular, although with a little less bulk. His hair was still mostly black, although now streaked with silver. And, the lines emanating from his eyes were deeper...both from years in the sun and age. *Age...the changer of all.*

Shaking his head, disgusted at the path his mind was wandering down, he brushed his teeth and flipped off the light. The master bedroom was not large but held everything that he needed to be comfortable, just like the rest of the house. He had pondered purchasing a king-sized bed when he moved in, but that would have taken up all the room. So, he settled for a queen size, giving plenty of space for his chest of drawers and a comfortable chair snuggled into the corner next to a floor lamp.

Climbing into bed, he appreciated the money spent on his firm mattress. Like the rest of him, his back was no longer that of a young man, and he discovered a too-soft mattress gave him no support and, therefore, no sleep. Lying in bed as he did every night, his mind cast back to what many would call the good old days. Men he had served with. Missions he had accomplished—the successful ones, as well as those that were not as successful.

Rolling over, he punched his pillow in an effort to plump it sufficiently. His eyes drifted to the window where he could see the starry night sky above the tree line. With a final sigh, he closed his eyes, willing sleep to come and, as with most nights, it did…eventually.

EARLY THE NEXT morning, Eric rounded the bend near the crystal, blue lake, his feet pounding a steady beat along the path. While landing in Vermont was completely by chance, it was through some research that he decided to live in this part of the state. The clear water of the lake and the surrounding forests gave a sense of peace and tranquility. He could sit on the deck of his cabin and enjoy the view or walk down the path from his home to the edge of the water where he kept his own kayak, which he often ventured out in.

If he gave it much thought, he would acknowledge that it was hard for a former Navy SEAL *not* to live near the water. The desire for an early morning swim, kayaking, or just being able to run along paths that meandered by the lake and through the woods was too strong for him to deny.

He pondered a swim that morning but decided on the run alone. Taking a deep breath of the fresh air, pain suddenly shot through his knee and he stumbled slightly. Forcing his pace to slow, he knew it did not make any sense to push harder than his knee would allow. There was nothing at stake here, no training time to meet, no place to be.

Refusing to focus on the pain, he continued to run along the path that now took him out of the thick evergreens and ran along the lake. In the distance he could see a few of the lodges that were built nearby, but it was too early in the morning for the vacationers to be out and about. With a last look toward the lake, he turned along the path that led back into the forest, appreciating the cool, crisp air that flowed over his body as he continued to run.

As he started the climb up the slight incline toward his cabin, the hairs on the back of his neck stood up. He slowed his pace and deviated from the path. Slipping silently through the forest surrounding his cabin, he made his way to a point where he could see the front of his house. The glint of sunlight off a vehicle's bumper caught his eye. Considering he parked his old pickup truck and SUV in the separate garage, he moved stealthily to gain a better view.

A large, black SUV with tinted windows sat in his driveway, parked near the front door. He observed no movement and was unable to discern anyone sitting inside. Moving around toward the back of his house, he stopped, seeing a man standing on his deck.

Black suit. White dress shirt. Black tie. Dark hair. Sunglasses. *Fuckin' hell.* He hated having his morning routine interrupted and, sure as hell, hated having someone standing on his back deck. But, as he made his way around to the stairs, he had to admit he was curious about his visitor.

Though his eyes were hidden by the sunglasses, it was clear the man was watching his ascent. Making it to the top of his deck, he stood arms akimbo, fists on his hips, and waited. The man did not speak. Neither did he. After a long minute of silence, he huffed out a frustrated breath. *This is bullshit.*

"You want to tell me who you are and why the hell you're standing on my deck?"

He watched as the man slid his sunglasses off before hooking them into his front suit pocket, still without saying a word. Taking the opportunity, he assessed the man fully. They were approximately the same height, both with dark hair streaks with silver, but whereas his stance was poised for the uncertainty of what might come, the other man stood ramrod straight and ease written on his face.

"I don't suppose you'd like to offer me a cup of coffee, would you?" the man finally asked.

He cocked his head to the side and quipped, "Perhaps an introduction might be warranted, before we decide to become best buddies over coffee."

The other man's lips quirked ever so slightly, and Eric was not sure if he was fighting a smile or if that was the best smile he could come up with.

"Branson. Silas Branson."

The man lifted his hand and, after a moment's consideration, Eric stepped forward, clasping it in his own. He had no idea what Silas Branson wanted with him, but with the requisite government vehicle in the front and the formal suit the man wore, he knew it had to be important. Besides, if he had to guess, he was looking at a fellow former SEAL.

With a head jerk to the side, he invited Silas to follow him as he moved through the sliding glass door. Walking toward the kitchen, he called over his shoulder, "Help yourself. Cups are in the cabinet. Coffee's already in the pot. Gimme five. Don't figure you want to have a conversation with me smelling like I do."

With that, he left Silas on his own and headed back to take a shower. Not waiting for the water to warm, he jumped in and rinsed off the sweat. Toweling off, he slid on boxers and jeans and pulled a T-shirt over his body. Scrubbing the towel over his head, he walked back to the living room.

Silas had taken off his suit jacket and it was carefully laid across the back of a chair, a cup of coffee sitting on the coffee table in front of it. The man was standing next to the fireplace, looking at the few framed photographs that he had placed there.

Rounding the kitchen counter, he pulled down his own mug and poured his coffee as well. Taking a sip, he put the mug on the counter and stood facing the living room, his arms in front of him with his palms flat against the surface, taking his weight.

"I don't mean to be a dick," he started, and Silas turned to look at him. "But I don't know you. I trust you enough to invite you into my home and offer you a cup of coffee, but unless you've got something to say to me, I think we can conclude this little meeting right now." He watched as Silas' lips quirked once more.

"Crash."

His brow lowered, but he remained silent.

"My call sign. Crash Branson."

"Ah," he muttered, his eyes widening as he recognized the name. Picking up his cup of coffee, he rounded the counter and motioned toward the chair while sitting down on the sofa. Silas took the silent invitation and sat down as well.

"See you've heard of me."

"Before my time, but yes. You had a fuckin' good reputation as a Lieutenant Commander. Heard you were picked up by DHS." He shrugged slightly and apologized, "'Fraid I didn't hear much after that."

Silas shook his head and waved his hand in a slight dismissive gesture. "Wouldn't have expected you to keep up." He glanced around the small, but comfortable room, before landing on the expansive view outside the window. "You've got a real nice place here. Quiet. Fuckin' gorgeous view. Nice place to retire."

ERIC LEANED BACK and settled comfortably. If a former SEAL Lieutenant Commander, now working for DHS, was sitting in his living room, it sure as hell was not about the view. But, Silas did not appear to be in a hurry and, since he had retired, he had nothing but time.

Turning his sharp gaze to him, Silas said, "I heard you helped out with a rescue last month."

That was true. He had been contacted by one of his former teammates who was now working for a private security firm. He had jumped at the chance to assist in a rescue and, having easy access to someone with a helicopter, it had been easy to fly to Boston for the mission.

"Rank—John Rankin was a good SEAL and is a good friend. Works for Lighthouse Security now. I was local, so it was easy to step in and assist."

Silas nodded, and asked, "You ever hear from Preacher?"

"Why do I get the feeling you already know the answers before you ask the questions?"

A slight smile crossed Silas' face. He was referring to Logan "Preacher" Bishop, another one of Eric's SEAL team members and an expert in logistics. Logan had been forced into medical retirement, same as him, several years ago. He had landed in one of the most unpopulated areas in the country—northern Montana—and flew birds for tourists and ski rescues.

He tried to read Silas' face, to judge whether he knew about Preacher's extracurricular activities, but he was not quite sure what to make of the man. And he sure as hell was not going to fill him in.

After another moment of silence, he found that he was no longer interested in playing whatever bullshit games Silas had in mind. "Once again, I don't mean to be a dick, but sitting here shooting the shit with you is not how I was going to spend my morning. I figure you're here for a reason…can we get to it?"

Silas leaned forward and picked up his coffee cup, taking a long sip before setting it back down. Lifting his gaze, he said with a grin, "How do you feel about pigs?"

Pigs? Fuckin' hell.

SEAL Together – Maryann Jordan

Here are the other books in the Silver SEALs Series:

1. *SEAL Love's Legacy* – **Sharon Hamilton**
2. *SEAL Together* – **Maryann Jordan**
3. *SEAL of Fortune* – **Becky McGraw**
4. *SEAL in Charge* – **Donna Michaels**
5. *SEAL in a Storm* – **KaLyn Cooper**
6. *SEAL Forever* – **Kris Michaels**
7. *SEAL Out of Water* – **Abbie Zanders**
8. *Sign, SEAL and Deliver* – **Geri Foster**
9. *SEAL Hard* – **J.m. Madden**
10. *SEAL Undercover* – **Desiree Holt**
11. *SEAL for Hire* – **Trish Loye**
12. *SEAL at Sunrise* – **Caitlyn O'Leary**
0. *SEAL Strong* – **Cat Johnson**

You can follow the Silver SEALs through the FB page and don't miss a thing!
facebook.com/SilverSEALsSeries

ABOUT THE AUTHOR

NYT and USA Today best-selling author Sharon Hamilton's award-winning Navy SEAL Brotherhood series have been a fan favorite from the day the first one was released. They've earned her the coveted Amazon author ranking of #1 in Romantic Suspense, Military Romance and Contemporary Romance categories, as well as in Gothic Romance for her Vampires of Tuscany and Guardian Angels. Her characters follow a sometimes rocky road to redemption through passion and true love.

Now that he's out of the Navy, Sharon can share with her readers that her son spent a decade as a Navy SEAL, and he's the inspiration for her books.

Her Golden Vampires of Tuscany are not like any vamps you've read about before, since they don't go to ground and can walk around in the full light of the sun.

Her Guardian Angels struggle with the human charges they are sent to save, often escaping their vanilla world of Heaven for the brief human one. You won't find any of these beings in any Sunday school class.

She lives in Sonoma County, California with her husband and her Doberman, Tucker. A lifelong organic gardener, when she's not writing, she's getting *verra verra* dirty in the mud, or wandering Farmers Markets looking for new Heirloom varieties of vegetables and flowers. She and her husband plan to cure their wanderlust (or make it worse) by traveling in their Diesel Class A Pusher, Romance Rider. Starting with this book, all her writing will be done on the road.

She loves hearing from her fans:
Sharonhamilton2001@gmail.com

Her website is:
sharonhamiltonauthor.com

Find out more about Sharon, her upcoming releases, appearances and news from her newsletter, **AND receive a free book** when you sign up for Sharon's newsletter.

Facebook:
facebook.com/SharonHamiltonAuthor

Twitter:
twitter.com/sharonlhamilton

Pinterest:
pinterest.com/AuthorSharonH

Google Plus:
plus.google.com/u/1/+SharonHamiltonAuthor/posts

BookBub:
bookbub.com/authors/sharon-hamilton

Youtube:

youtube.com/channel/UCDInkxXFpXp_4Vnq08ZxMBQ

Soundcloud:

soundcloud.com/sharon-hamilton-1

Sharon Hamilton's Rockin' Romance Readers:

facebook.com/groups/sealteamromance

Sharon Hamilton's Goodreads Group:

goodreads.com/group/show/199125-sharon-hamilton-readers-group

Visit Sharon's Online Store:

sharon-hamilton-author.myshopify.com

Join Sharon's Review Teams:

eBook Reviews:

sharonhamiltonassistant@gmail.com

Audio Reviews:

sharonhamiltonassistant@gmail.com

Life is one fool thing after another.
Love is two fool things after each other.

REVIEWS

PRAISE FOR THE
GOLDEN VAMPIRES OF TUSCANY SERIES

"Well to say the least I was thoroughly surprise. I have read many Vampire books, from Ann Rice to Kym Grosso and few other Authors, so yes I do like Vampires, not the super scary ones from the old days, but the new ones are far more interesting far more human then one can remember. I found Honeymoon Bite a totally engrossing book, I was not able to put it down, page after page I found delight, love, understanding, well that is until the bad bad Vamp started being really bad. But seeing someone love another person so much that they would do anything to protect them, well that had me going, then well there was more and for a while I thought it was the end of a beautiful love story that spanned not only time but, spanned Italy and California. Won't divulge how it ended, but I did shed a few tears after screaming but Sharon Hamilton did not let me down, she took me on amazing trip that I loved, look forward to reading another Vampire book of hers."

"An excellent paranormal romance that was exciting,

romantic, entertaining and very satisfying to read. It had me anticipating what would happen next many times over, so much so I could not put it down and even finished it up in a day. The vampires in this book were different from your average vampire, but I enjoy different variations and changes to the same old stuff. It made for a more unpredictable read and more adventurous to explore! Vampire lovers, any paranormal readers and even those who love the romance genre will enjoy Honeymoon Bite."

"This is the first non-Seal book of this author's I have read and I loved it. There is a cast-like hierarchy in this vampire community with humans at the very bottom and Golden vampires at the top. Lionel is a dark vampire who are servants of the Goldens. Phoebe is a Golden who has not decided if she will remain human or accept the turning to become a vampire. Either way she and Lionel can never be together since it is forbidden.

I enjoyed this story and I am looking forward to the next installment."

"A hauntingly romantic read. Old love lost and new love found. Family, heart, intrigue and vampires. Grabbed my attention and couldn't put down. Would definitely recommend."

PRAISE FOR THE
SEAL BROTHERHOOD SERIES

"Fans of Navy SEAL romance, I found a new author to feed your addiction. Finely written and loaded delicious with moments, Sharon Hamilton's storytelling satisfies like a thick bar of chocolate." —Marliss Melton, bestselling author of the *Team Twelve* Navy SEALs series

"Sharon Hamilton does an EXCELLENT job of fitting all the characters into a brotherhood of SEALS that may not be real but sure makes you feel that you have entered the circle and security of their world. The stories intertwine with each book before...and each book after and THAT is what makes Sharon Hamilton's SEAL Brotherhood Series so very interesting. You won't want to put down ANY of her books and they will keep you reading into the night when you should be sleeping. Start with this book...and you will not want to stop until you've read the whole series and then...you will be waiting for Sharon to write the next one." (5 Star Review)

"Kyle and Christy explode all over the pages in this first book, *[Accidental SEAL]*, in a whole new series of SEALs. If the twist and turns don't get your heart jumping, then maybe the suspense will. This is a must read for those that are looking for love and adventure with a little sloppy love thrown in for good measure." (5 Star Review)

PRAISE FOR THE
BAD BOYS OF SEAL TEAM 3 SERIES

"I love reading this series! Once you start these books, you can hardly put them down. The mix of romance and suspense keeps you turning the pages one right after another! Can't wait until the next book!" (5 Star Review)

"I love all of Sharon's Seal books, but [SEAL's Code] may just be her best to date. Danny and Luci's journey is filled with a wonderful insight into the Native American life. It is a love story that will fill you with warmth and contentment. You will enjoy Danny's journey to become a SEAL and his reasons for it. Good job Sharon!" (5 Star Review)

PRAISE FOR THE
BAND OF BACHELORS SERIES

"[Lucas] was the first book in the Band of Bachelors series and it was a phenomenal start. I loved how we got to see the other SEALs we all love and we got a look at Lucas and Marcy. They had an instant attraction, and their love was very intense. This book had it all, suspense, steamy romance, humor, everything you want in a riveting, outstanding read. I can't wait to read the next book in this series." (5 Star Review)

PRAISE FOR THE
TRUE BLUE SEALS SERIES

"Keep the tissues box nearby as you read *True Blue SEALs: Zak* by Sharon Hamilton. I imagine more than I wish to that the circumstances surrounding Zak and Amy are all too real for returning military personnel and their families. Ms. Hamilton has put us right in the middle of struggles and successes that these two high school sweethearts endure. I have read several of Sharon Hamilton's military romances but will say this is the most emotionally intense of the ones that I have read. This is a well-written, realistic story with authentic characters that will have you rooting for them and proud of those who serve to keep us safe. This is an author who writes amazing stories that you love and cry with the characters. Fans of Jessica Scott and Marliss Melton will want to add Sharon Hamilton to their list of realistic military romance writers." (5 Star Review)

56333176R00167

Made in the USA
Columbia, SC
23 April 2019